Cameron, Eleanor
    A mystery for Mr. Bass.   Illus. by
Leonard Shortall.   Little, Brown [1960]
    229 p.

        Title

BY ELEANOR CAMERON

A MYSTERY FOR MR. BASS

A Mystery for Mr. Bass

A Mushroom Planet Book

by ELEANOR CAMERON

Illustrated by Leonard Shortall

An Atlantic Monthly Press Book

Little, Brown and Company · Boston · Toronto

LIBRARY OF CONGRESS CATALOG CARD NO. 60–9344

Ninth Printing

The lines from JIM JAY by Walter de la Mare are used by permission of the Literary Trustees of Walter de la Mare and The Society of
Authors.

ATLANTIC–LITTLE, BROWN BOOKS
ARE PUBLISHED BY
LITTLE, BROWN AND COMPANY
IN ASSOCIATION WITH
THE ATLANTIC MONTHLY PRESS

Published simultaneously in Canada
by Little, Brown & Company (Canada) Limited

PRINTED IN THE UNITED STATES OF AMERICA

This book is for David Lawsky, in happy remembrance of the day we met in the Boys' and Girls' Department of the Los Angeles Public Library.

Contents

PART ONE

The Rune of the Spore People

CHAPTER 1

The Last Straw

On a narrow, winding road high above the ocean near Pacific Grove, California, a small green car was humming along around the bends just a little bit too fast. Prewytt Brumblydge, its driver, was thinking, and of course he was thinking about his Brumblydge Theory of the Universe. So when his left front tire went *bang!* and the little car wobbled and swerved violently across the center line of that two-lane road, only his hands knew what to do. At once they gripped the steering wheel with all their strength. But instead of pressing and then releasing the foot brake, his foot jammed down too hard and too long, whereupon the car slewed off in the opposite direction, headed straight for that steep drop above the ocean.

"Ah-h-h-h!" cried Prewytt in horror, and closed his eyes tight so as not to have to watch his last moment swooping and spinning past.

Just in time, however, the car scrunched to a halt,

but Prewytt was certain that his right front tire must be resting on the extreme edge of that fifty-foot cliff at the side of the road.

He sank back, pale and trembling, his heart thudding, and brushed a weak hand across his forehead, which was all bedewed with sweat. He was rather a plump, short man, usually very brisk and overflowing with energy and purpose. But he had not been feeling at all well today, not at all the master of himself. So now, on top of what had just happened, his face looked yellowish-gray with scarcely a touch of green in it. Had he been in good health, that touch would have been distinctly noticeable. For Prewytt, like his good friend Tyco Bass, the famous astronomer, was an earthen Basidiumite or spore person, and all spore people tend to show an underlying hint of greenishness in their complexions.

Prewytt held out a hand, saw that it shook, exclaimed *"Tchk!"* and then got out on rubbery legs to have a look. Sure enough, the right front wheel *was* resting on the very edge of the road that fell away steeply into the ravine. Another few inches, Prewytt saw, and he would have been hurled into oblivion.

"But this is getting to be too much," he whispered to himself. "One piece of bad luck, one narrow escape after another, and if they keep up they will be

4

the death of me." He lifted his head and stared out over the sunny Pacific visible through the tall masts of Monterey pines. "What can be happening? What can it mean? Foolish, perhaps — but I am really beginning to be frightened."

For a moment longer he brooded in silence. Then, still looking deeply concerned, he went round to the rear of the car, unlocked the trunk, took off his jacket, folded it neatly, and commenced to unbolt the spare tire from its rack.

CHAPTER 2

A Certain Uneasiness

Bʏ ᴛʜᴇ time Prewytt got back to 5 Thallo Street, where he had been staying with Tyco Bass for the past few weeks, the sky had completely changed from soft blue to a lowering, ominous gray. But he was feeling far too wretched to notice, nor did he pay any attention to the sea gulls creaking and crying overhead, nor pause to wonder at these out-of-season signs of a coming storm.

"Mr. Brumblydge!" shouted David Topman, a slim, brown-haired boy, who was pedaling his bike for all he was worth along Thallo Street, with Chuck Masterson, shorter and sturdier, racing along behind. "Mr. Brumblydge, have you had any answers to your ads for Brumblium meteorites yet?"

Prewytt, who had just stepped out of his car, went wearily over and leaned on the white picket fence where there was a notice nailed up which read Sᴏᴄɪᴇᴛʏ ᴏғ Yᴏᴜɴɢ Aѕᴛʀᴏɴᴏᴍᴇʀѕ ᴀɴᴅ Sᴛᴜᴅᴇɴᴛѕ ᴏғ Sᴘᴀᴄᴇ Tʀᴀᴠᴇʟ. Now David and Chuck swung off their bikes, and at the same time a little man no taller than Prewytt or the boys, frail-looking and wearing an old gray gardening coat and elastic-sided boots, came out from behind some bushes in the garden. He seemed, by the few wisps of hair on his large, balding head, to be much older than Prewytt. Yet there was something exceedingly merry and youthful in his expression, and his brown eyes sparkled as he came forward. This was David's and Chuck's good friend, Mr. Bass.

However, the minute he saw Prewytt's face he stopped. Wiping crumbs of rich, dark earth from his hands (for he had been pulling weeds out of the chrysanthemum border), he studied the other little man anxiously.

"Why, Prewytt," he said, "I don't believe I've ever seen you look quite so seedy. Aren't you feeling well? And you seem all rumpled somehow." No wonder Mr. Bass commented on this, for Prewytt was usually the neatest person imaginable, one of those people who seem always to have come right from the tailor's.

"Golly, Mr. Brumblydge," said Chuck, standing there with his dark eyes fixed on Prewytt's face, "you look *awful!*" Chuck never could help coming out with the bald truth.

"I think maybe you've got a fever," announced

David thoughtfully. "Your color's so sort of peculiar."

"I don't know," Prewytt muttered. "Terribly strange — never sick in my life —" He took out a beautifully laundered white linen handkerchief and mopped his forehead. "No word's come yet, I suppose, Tyco, from any rock-hounds or museums?" Regretfully Mr. Bass shook his head. "Well, then," went on Prewytt, "it looks as if I'm going to have to depend entirely on your friends up on Basidium for my Brumblium. Just think of it, Tyco: a whole planet made almost entirely of Brumblium, and your Mushroom People aren't doing a thing with it but just living on it —"

"And you could do so much!" finished David, grinning at him.

At first David and Chuck had worried mightily over the idea of Prewytt's getting his precious metal from Basidium, their secret planet. Basidium was a small world only fifty thousand miles out from earth, which Mr. Bass had discovered by means of a special lens attached to his telescope, and which astronomers of earth had not yet so much as dreamed of.

"But, boys, remember that Prewytt is a spore person just as I am and as the people of Basidium are," Tyco had pointed out at the time Prewytt was to be let in on the secret. "I've known him for many, many years and I assure you we can trust him with our knowledge of the Mushroom Planet. Besides, he really must get ahead with that invention of his, and he can't do it without his special metal. I'm absolutely certain his Brumblitron could be of the greatest service to earth, especially if he can get several of them going."

Prewytt's invention was a black box covered with lead, and had many wires going from it up to a huge, web-shaped antenna. The antenna, in turn, captured B-rays, and these, by their action on the metal, Brumblium, could transform salt water into fresh. So of course the parched places of the earth would welcome Brumblitrons by the dozens. Thus far, Prewytt had been able to find only two pieces of his rare metal in the form of meteorites, but both had been lost when Prewytt had had to destroy his first Brumblitron to keep it from exploding.

Now Mr. Bass said to Prewytt, "I signaled Ta and Cousin Theo on Basidium not half an hour ago, just to find how matters stand. And Cousin Theo flashed back that a final decision about your getting the metal from them will be made by Ta and his subjects two weeks from today."

"Two *weeks!*" burst out Prewytt in impatient dismay. "Why, I could have a whole Brumblitron built in that time. In fact, I think I'll —"

"*I* think," returned Tyco with sudden firmness,

10

"that you had better get into bed at once," and he came out and took Prewytt's arm. "Come along, David and Chuck, you give him a hand, too. You know, Prewytt, the world's had to wait all these centuries for your invention, so it isn't going to hurt it to wait a bit longer for deserts to be turned into green gardens —"

"And for my fossil-dating process, Tyco!" reminded Prewytt eagerly, his round face lighting, sick as he was, while he allowed himself to be led through the gate. "That's the beauty of it, don't you see — there's no *end* to what the Brumblitron can do!"

They helped Mr. Brumblydge along the shaded path that led to Tyco's small white house, which was almost buried in trees and above which could be seen the round dome of his little observatory. Five minutes later Prewytt was sitting on the edge of the bed in Tyco's comfortable bedroom, and Tyco was helping him into a clean pair of pajamas. Chuck was getting out an extra blanket and David was filling a hot-water bottle, for Prewytt, in spite of his fever, had begun to shiver so hard that his teeth were chattering. Then they tucked him in.

"I think that we had better call David's father, Prewytt," said Mr. Bass. "I'm sure I'd feel better if you'd have a doctor —"

11

But Prewytt said that he didn't *need* a doctor. He didn't *want* a doctor, not even David's father. This was only a touch of influenza, he said, and he would be as fit as a flea by the next morning and then he and Tyco could get on with their discussion of B-rays and the part they played in his Theory of the Universe.

"One m-more thing — T-Tyco, d-do you s-suppose your C-Cousin Theo c-could — m-maybe p-persuade Ta to —"

"Now, Prewytt, you just stop fretting and go to sleep. There's nothing any of us can do to hasten matters on Basidium. We must be patient." And Tyco turned and herded the boys out of the bedroom, but left the door open a crack so that they could hear if Prewytt needed anything.

"Poor Mr. Brumblydge," said David in a low voice. "Two weeks is an awfully long time — Chuck and I just can't wait to start out for Basidium again. But, golly, the space ship isn't in good enough shape yet for another journey."

"Indeed it isn't, David," returned Mr. Bass. "I have a great deal of work still to do on it. As for the message from the Mushroom Planet, this decision as to whether Prewytt can take Brumblium from there isn't up to Ta alone, simply because he is King of the Mushroom People. It's up to his subjects as well.

12

Now — come and sit down while I tell you something."

But at this moment Tyco apparently noticed the dimness of the living room, for he went over to the window and peered out. Chuck and David followed, and, looking up, David saw that the clouds were darkening and scudding before a rising wind and the sea gulls still wheeled in wide circles uttering piercing cries of "Creeee-ee, creee-eeeee-ee —"

"But if there *is* going to be a storm," murmured Mr. Bass, "it would seem very unusual for this time of year. When have we ever had a storm in September? Well, let us turn on the lamps." Now he settled himself, a small, slight figure, in his favorite armchair, and the boys sat opposite him on the couch. "What I have to tell you is this — you heard me say that Ta's decision will come two weeks from today. But, my dear friends, I shall not be here to know of it."

"Oh, *Mr. Bass!*" exclaimed Chuck in bitter disappointment, and David's gray eyes and the expression of his pale brown face showed what he felt.

"I am as sorry as you, Chuck. But you see," continued Tyco, "I promised the Ancient Ones faithfully that if I were allowed to leave my new home in the Galaxy M 81 in Ursa Major at the time Prewytt almost blew himself up with the Brumblitron, I

13

would return at pre-*cise*ly whatever hour they set. And that hour falls eleven days from today, on Tuesday, September 28, at seven in the evening, earth time —"

"So soon!" mourned David. Ever since Mr. Bass had first discovered Basidium and made it possible for the boys to take off in their own space ship to visit the little planet, he had been their closest friend. He had been living here on earth at the time of his discovery, but soon afterwards the Ancient Ones decreed that he should leave earth and make his home in a solar system in another galaxy. Twice since then he had returned when David and Chuck had needed him most, and this last time they'd hoped he might stay. But now, only eleven days left! Why, that was no time at all.

"So I shall leave everything in your hands," Tyco went on, studying their faces. "If Ta decides that you two boys shall go alone to Basidium and leave Prewytt behind, it will be a hard blow for him. But it will be up to you to get the Brumblium and bring it back safely, and to let no Earth Person learn where it came from. For the time has not yet arrived when the world may know of the Mushroom Planet."

"We understand, Mr. Bass," David assured him. "It's still a secret, and *nobody's* going to get it out of us."

14

"Good, David. And meanwhile I shall work every moment I possibly can on the space ship, so that when I have to leave, it will be completely ready for your journey."

When he had to leave! A ripple went down David's arms, for Mr. Bass needed no space ship. He had only to think of himself in that far Galaxy of M 81, which is seven hundred and thirty-four and a half million light-years away, and he would arrive there instantly. When he traveled, time and distance had no meaning for Mr. Bass.

A little later, after the boys had started for home, Tyco stood on his porch looking up at the sky. A strange uneasiness, or unrest, had been creeping over him for the past two hours or so, and now this uneasiness seemed somehow increased by the sullen grayness of the air. It had a kind of steely-blue tone in it, he thought, that made the green of the garden look almost phosphorescent — a livid, threatening green.

There is going to be such a storm, he told himself, listening to the turmoil of the upper air and then turning and going in — such a storm as the Monterey Peninsula has never known . . . and I have the oddest notion, Tyco, that there is something here you should understand.

Once inside, he went right to the steep and narrow stairs that led to his observatory, those stairs that had a very special meaning for Chuck and David because they would never forget the excitement that had filled them when Tyco first led them up.

Now Mr. Bass settled himself at his desk and turned on the lamp. In this room his homemade telescope stood, pointing up to the domed, ridged roof. Those almost-magical paintings which he had done of the planets and their satellites hung on the walls; and his astronomy books, as well as volumes on numberless other subjects, filled the cases beneath.

On the floor opposite his desk stood one of his remarkable lanterns, whose soft, cool, silvery-green rays were capable of flashing messages across fifty thousand miles of space. At this moment it was turned to "receive," so that if his Cousin Theo on Basidium wanted to tell him something it would immediately light up with the long and short flashes of the message. There was a lantern in every room as well as in Tyco's cellar workroom, so that wherever he or the boys were, they would know at once if Theo was speaking to them.

Finally, there was a safe set into the wall near his desk which held the objects Tyco and the boys treasured most. Among other things (some jewels from Basidium and a necklace Ta had given David and

Chuck) was the marvelous Stroboscopic Polarizing
Filter. This was an invention of Tyco's own which,
when fitted snugly over the eyepiece of the telescope,
had brought Basidium swimming into view where

no heavenly body was supposed to be. For though the Mushroom Planet is a satellite of earth's only fifty thousand miles away, it is invisible when viewed without the Filter, which is why human astronomers know nothing of it. Here in the safe was also kept Tyco's long ledger, which he called *Random Jottings* and in which he wrote every day in his own language, the language of Basidium.

Now Tyco took out the ledger and opened it. All was quiet in that domed, lamp-lit, cozy room. But no sooner had his pen begun its rapid scratching across the page than such a bolt of thunder crashed through the skies above Thallo Street that it seemed surely Tyco's house and every house in the neighborhood must be crushed beneath it. It rumbled into the earth like a hammer blow of the gods. And then the rain descended as if the heavens had opened and the final deluge had come.

CHAPTER 3

Surprise!

Tyco was right about the storm. Never had the Monterey Peninsula known such continuous violence, such a lashing, torrential downpour.

But curiously enough, by Saturday morning the storm clouds had vanished completely and the weather became, if anything, warmer than usual. The whole Peninsula basked in the sun, the air was filled with the fragrance of damp earth and bark and pine needles, and the ocean was three shades deeper than the sky.

Mr. Bass worked late and hard during that stormy night going over the steps of Prewytt's fossil-dating process, for he was troubled about it. He was quite sure there was something wrong somewhere. Several times he had gone in to see how Prewytt was getting along, but had heard nothing except occasional tossings and mutterings, a moan or two, and several sharp snores. Then Tyco himself had dropped off to

19

sleep on the couch in the living room and had not stirred until this moment.

Seven-thirty, announced the clock on the mantel, chiming once for the half-hour. Tyco tiptoed over, care-ful-ly pushed back the bedroom door — and peeked in.

The bed was empty!

"*What?*" cried Tyco in utter amazement. "But how could he — how could he possibly have gotten past me, sleeping as lightly as I do?" Then he turned and saw that a window, which had not been up last night, stood wide open. Mr. Brumblydge's suitcase was gone and there was a note, Tyco noticed, on the pillow.

DEAR TYCO:

It is now five in the morning and I am feeling somewhat better. But in case I should come down with a really serious case of influenza (and I wouldn't be a bit surprised, for you may have noticed I've had quite a run of bad luck lately), I want to be out of the way so that you and the boys won't get it. Mrs. Lilly Cuttle, my landlady up at San Julian, will keep an eye on me, and I do hope she'll be willing to turn down that infernal television of hers.

Thank you for your hospitality, Tyco. We had some good talks, didn't we, even though you still refuse to admit that brumblic pentathermonuclearcosmicdiheliumite is a better space-ship fuel than atomic tritetramethylbenzacarbonethylene. One of these days we shall see.

Your old friend,
P. B.

"Oh, Prewytt!" Tyco exclaimed aloud to the empty room. "What a foolish thing to do with influenza

coming on — or already come, I should say! I declare! Let's see: seven-thirty — so if he was able to keep driving, he should be home by now. But I think I'd better phone just to be certain."

Yes, said Mrs. Cuttle, Mr. Brumblydge was indeed home, *and* safe in his bed, *and* very sick. What a *silly* man he had been to drive all that way! He kept going on about a blowout and about some mistake he had made, a *terrible* mistake, he kept saying over and over. But she couldn't understand anything else because he was in such a high fever. No, there wasn't a thing Mr. Bass could do, thank you all the same. She'd already called the doctor.

Tyco hung up, feeling deeply depressed. Was it a mistake in the fossil-dating process Prewytt meant? But surely it wasn't as serious as all that. A *terrible* mistake! What an odd way to put it.

And he did wish, Tyco thought to himself, that this sharp, puzzling uneasiness would go away — a kind of foreboding, it was. He couldn't fathom it, yet he kept feeling he should be able to, that there was probably some perfectly clear reason for it right under his nose if only he could bring the right words or hints together. Ah, but he couldn't, and so, heaving a sigh, he padded off in his carpet slippers to put the bacon on for breakfast.

22

CHAPTER 4

Mr. Bass Makes a Wager

As for David and Chuck, they made the best possible use of Saturday's fine weather. Of course they phoned Tyco that morning to ask if they could help him with the space ship, but when he told them he had some very difficult, touchy wiring to do, they said they had another project they might just as well get on with.

About four that afternoon they appeared at the door of Tyco's cellar workroom with their bikes, and they were a sight to behold. Their sneakers and the legs of their jeans up to the knees were covered with dried mud, and their faces and shirts were streaked with it. Chuck, as usual, had gotten himself into the worst mess, but both seemed extremely pleased with themselves.

"Why, boys," Tyco exclaimed, turning from the space ship and laying down his tools, "you look as if you've been digging at the bottom of a well!"

They grinned, and Chuck at once began trying to untie a big, stained bandanna handkerchief. However, the cloth was damp and he had pulled the knot so tight that he was having quite a hard time with it.

"We found something, Mr. Bass," he said, his eyes bright with excitement. "O' course, they're just some old bones. You prob'ly won't think they're very interesting."

"We even thought maybe we wouldn't bother to bring 'em," said David, but his eyes were shining.

Now at last Chuck conquered the knot, and out of the bandana, with the air of a magician producing a rabbit, he tumbled the bones into Mr. Bass's hands.

There they lay, cupped in his slender palms with his long fingers curving over: three pieces, not very large. One was a lower jawbone with four teeth still in place. Another was triangular with what looked like a hillock in the middle, and the remaining one was thin and curved, with a narrow, shelflike ridge near one edge.

What was most curious about them was the color. They were brown, as bones that have been buried in earth for a long time are apt to be. But combined with this was a strange, underlying hint of greenishness, so that they looked as if they had been fashioned of bronze. And they were so fine and delicate, they might almost have been carved by some skilled

24

artist who had rubbed and polished them to a smooth, satiny finish.

For a moment Mr. Bass did not speak (David had an idea he *could* not speak), but simply stared. Then at last:

"My dear boys, only some old bones, you say! *Only some old bones!*"

"Well, aren't they, Mr. Bass?" asked Chuck. "They're not fossils, are they?" he ventured.

"Yes, Chuck, they *are* fossils — indeed they are —"

"Were they the bones of an Indian child? They're so small."

"No, Chuck, not an Indian child," returned Mr. Bass quietly.

Now he took the bones over to his workbench and arranged them in a pattern with the jawbone at the bottom, the triangular piece at the side above it, and at the top the thin, curved piece with the shelflike ridge.

"All parts of a human skull, you see," he murmured, "the triangular piece with the little hillock being the cheekbone, and the thin, curved piece being a part of the forehead. The shelf is the brow ridge."

But my brows don't stick out nearly that much, flashed into David's mind, and he ran his fingers over them just to be certain.

"Will we get a prize, do you think, Mr. Bass? Are they valuable? Will the museum want them?"

"The museum, David?" asked Tyco, puzzled. "What museum?"

"The Peninsula Museum of Science," broke in Chuck eagerly. "You see, it's giving a prize for the best contribution to its new wing, the Hall of Man, and one of the prizes is for kids up to thirteen. So when we found out about it, we phoned Dr. Shellworthy right away to ask where we could dig, and he said why not try the bottom of his garden first of all. He said he'd found part of an Indian shell necklace there once, in the cliff, and farther along a piece of an old Indian bowl. But *he* never found any bones. Mrs. Shellworthy wasn't home when we went up to tell her."

Tyco perched himself on his stool and turned a sharp, attentive look upon David and Chuck.

"Tell me, please," he said, "pre-*cise*ly where you found these bones."

"Well, two of them," replied David, "we found at the foot of the cliff, maybe washed out by the storm. Because they were right at the foot, but in different places, sort of half-buried with only parts sticking up. But the jawbone we found in the cliff. We spotted it first, and it looked as if a lot of earth had washed away around it —"

26

"So that was why we hunted on the ground," interrupted Chuck, "because the jawbone looked as if it was just about to be washed down, so we thought some other bones might have."

"Will we get a prize, Mr. Bass?" pressed David anxiously.

Tyco turned to him, and there was a most peculiar light in his eyes.

"David," he said, "if you were to hand these pieces to the curator, he could not find a prize worthy of them, for there is not a museum in the world that has anything that could even begin to compare with them. *They are absolutely priceless!*"

"But, Mr. Bass," burst out Chuck, "how do you know they're priceless?"

Tyco gave him a quick smile.

"Let me show you something," he said.

Whereupon Mr. Bass, to the boys' wonderment, went over and turned off the bubbles of light that had sent their cool, clear glow into every corner of the cellar workroom. And lo and behold! — another glow, not silvery-golden like that of the bubbles that hung under the rafters, but rather resembling the strange, greenish-silver fox fire that came from Mr. Bass's lanterns, rose from the bench where lay the bones.

They were bathed in their own light. Pale, green-

ish-silver pale, glimmered the astounded faces of David and Chuck, and on the elfish face of Mr. Bass was revealed an expression which David, when he glanced up, could not read.

"Beneath my flesh, too," said Mr. Bass softly, "could they be uncovered in the dark, lie bones filled with light as these are — but a brighter, more vivid light, because I am a living being. Beneath the flesh of all earthen spore people, or Mycetians, as they call themselves, as well as the Mushroom People of Basidium, lies the hidden light.

"For we are indeed one race, and the passing of ages cannot rob our bones of this sign, the seal of oneness, the silver-green glow. It dims with time, yet it remains." Mr. Bass paused, and the boys were silent, too dumfounded to speak.

"As for the age of the bones," Mr. Bass went on musingly, "I could use Prewytt's method to test them — except that I have no Brumblitron and no Brumblium, and I do not think his method can be trusted. I could use carbon-dating, which the whole world recognizes, but these bones are too old for that. I could use fluorine-dating, but that would not give me a precise date. Therefore, this very night, I shall use a certain process of my own."

David, his gray eyes still held by that serene and ghostly light, laid a hand on Mr. Bass's arm.

"Tell us," he said, "how old you think the bones will turn out to be."

Tyco did not answer for a moment, but then:

"I will wager, David, that they belonged to a Mycetian, one of my own spore people, who lived on earth at least half a million years ago."

"Half a million years ago!" breathed David and Chuck together.

"Yes, my friends, but there are two things about your finding the bones here that are a complete mystery to me. First of all, I cannot understand how they came to be lying in or at the foot of a cliff on the western coast of this continent when no remains of early man have so far been found in either North or South America that have been proved to be older than fifty thousand years — and your find is probably at least ten times older than that!"

"And second of all, Mr. Bass?" urged David.

"Second of all," replied Tyco, "the bones of Mycetians are supposed to lie in only one secret place —"

"What place?" questioned Chuck eagerly. "Where is it?"

"It is in Wales, the original home of the Mycetians, and it is just below Harlech, where there is a long line of mysterious stone steps, which everybody calls the Roman Steps, that wind inland for almost two miles. But those stone steps were not built by the Romans. They were there centuries before the Romans came, and it is at the top of those steps, since time immemorial, that my people have always been buried, at the foot of a craggy little mountain."

"Then, Mr. Bass," asked Chuck, "has that burying

ground been there for half a million years, do you suppose?"

"I don't know, Chuck. It's possible. But it is a strange thing — I have never heard of any of our bones being turned up anywhere else on earth. Wait until we talk to Austin Shellworthy and you shall see."

The boys had gone and now the workroom was still. Mr. Bass sat at his bench with the bones before him, the features of his small face cast into odd peaks and shadows by their pale glimmering. Behind him, the space ship shone faintly, long and slender, its nose diminishing to a needle point and the four blades around the rocket exhaust just visible in the darkness at the far end of the cellar. It seemed poised there, hovering above its carrier by means of some secret power of its own.

Mr. Bass picked up the bones and cradled them in his hands. They were cool to the touch — their light gave no heat.

What do they hold in store for us? he silently asked himself. Has the discovery of these bones anything to do with that mysterious and sudden storm — and perhaps with this strange foreboding of mine? How can this be possible? Yet it may be, for the bones, the storm, and the foreboding have all come at the same time and each, in its own way, is puzzling and unexplainable. Yes, there is something here I must understand — with only ten days left and the space ship still to be worked on. So short a while in which to do so much!

CHAPTER 5

The Rune

Very late the next afternoon, if you had looked in at the dusty window, well hidden by bushes, of Mr. Bass's cellar, you would have beheld the unearthly greenish-silver glow spreading into the darkness around the three Mycetian bones on the workbench. Above them hung the ghostly faces of Mr. Bass, Chuck and David, and tall, thin Dr. Austin Shellworthy, who had come over from the College of the Peninsula. He seemed positively overcome with astonishment.

"I can't believe it, Tyco!" he was saying. "And you say that this giving off of light is in the nature of the bones themselves and not due to any element or chemical they might have absorbed from the soil?"

"That's right, Austin. Any Mycetian bones I have ever seen glowed in just this manner when they were turned up in the earth of our secret burying ground at the foot of the mountain in Wales."

"Glowed in the earth of your secret burying

33

ground," murmured Dr. Shellworthy. "And they have never been found anywhere else? Certainly I've never heard of any such bones as these being discovered anywhere. But five hundred thousand years old, Tyco! *Half a million years!* And to be found *here!* How many times did you test them?"

"Five, and each time with pre-*cise*ly the same results."

Dr. Shellworthy stared at him.

"If you are right, Tyco," he said in a low voice, "then it looks to me as if somebody must have *put* the bones in the cliff. And in that case it may be that we have a hoax on our hands."

"A hoax, Austin!" exclaimed Mr. Bass. "*Tchk!* Now I hadn't thought of that. You see, as far back as my people have any records at all, as far back as we have been able to read the hints and signs of our ancient past, we find that we have always gone home to die in Wales or, if that was not possible, our bones were taken or sent home. Therefore, if someone *brought* these bones from Wales, and buried them in that cliff for a joke, or indeed for any reason, I can only say he was either ignorant or very courageous."

"Courageous, Mr. Bass!" cried David. "But why do you say that?"

"Because, David," replied Tyco in the gravest tone, "there is a Mycetian rune, not rhymed in earliest times, but having become rhymed through much use. A rune, you know, boys, can be either one of the letters of the old Norse or Finnish alphabets, or a piece of their earliest poetry, and the word also has a meaning of magic. This is the rune:

> *Remember the ancient words of Wyrd,*
> *Carved at Llanbedr by a hand afeard —*
> *That blackest misfortune shall follow him hard*
> *Who robs our graves near the mountain's guard.*
> *And he, thus cursed, must return our bones,*
> *Who would free himself of the rune of the stones."*

" 'Blackest misfortune,' " breathed David. "Oh, I see — that's what you meant by courage. Because somebody would have had to steal them."

"What's 'Wyrd,' Mr. Bass?" asked Chuck, and he pronounced it "Weird," as Tyco had done.

"That's the old name, Chuck, among the early Britons, for Fate."

Now Dr. Shellworthy got up from Tyco's high stool, where he had perched himself, and walked rapidly up and down beside the space ship. He had given it a startled glance when he first came into the cellar, and no doubt would have examined it and inquired about it with the keenest interest had not the matter of the bones been of the utmost importance to him.

"Tyco," he said, shoving his hands into his pockets,

"why do you call your people Mycetians? I, an anthropologist, have never in my life heard of a Mycetian."

David held his breath, wondering just how much Mr. Bass would be willing to tell.

"I am a Mycetian, Austin — and the middle name of each one of us is always Mycetes, which has to do with fungi and mushrooms, which of course reproduce by spores. Therefore, you see, we are also spore people."

"*Spore people — Mycetians!*" burst out Austin Shellworthy. "I've heard of spore people, Tyco. But, Great Scott, I've always put them in a class with trolls and gnomes and goblins. And do you mean to tell me — do you mean to stand there and tell me that *you, my old friend, are one of them?*" Poor Dr. Shellworthy looked as if he had an idea he might be dreaming, but Mr. Bass nodded, his eyes twinkling. "Well, Tyco — have you always called yourselves Mycetians?"

"Only as far back as we, in Wales, had any knowledge of the Greek language, Austin. Because the word Mycetes, as you know, comes from the Greek word *mykētos*, meaning fungus. But we have an unbelievably ancient past which goes back thousands of years before that."

Dr. Shellworthy did not speak for a moment. Then

he sank onto the stool again and studied the little man who stood serenely before him with wide, innocent brown eyes.

"Tyco," he said finally, "will you please tell me all about the Mycetians? Because I have the strongest feeling that I must be absolutely clear about them if I am to help solve the mystery of this find."

CHAPTER 6

The Mycetian League

B y the pale light of the Mycetian bones, little Mr. Bass's face appeared to grow fainter in outline for a moment as though, thought David, he had gone off somewhere to decide in private what he might say. Then he looked at Austin Shellworthy, his eyes brightening.

"I shall be happy to tell you all that is permitted, Austin."

"All that is permitted," repeated Dr. Shellworthy, frowning slightly. "But I don't understand — permitted by whom?"

"Ah, well, we shall come to that," smiled Tyco. "First of all, you must know," he began, wrapping his gardening coat about him and interlacing his long, delicate fingers, "that there are only around five and a half thousand spore people in the whole world, among all the millions of human beings, so it is no wonder that you know little or nothing of us, Austin, and that whatever you heard, you thought was fable.

39

Of these five thousand, most live in the British Isles, and of the British Mycetians, most live in Wales, our ancestral home. The cool, damp, green, misty places we love the best —"

Cool, damp, green, and misty like Basidium, thought David.

"Now, in Wales," went on Tyco, "we have always had magic attributed to us. Wales is full of magic, you know — there are Welsh who still believe in it, particularly out in the countryside. And of course the early tales of the spore people have become mixed with stories of elves and pixies, those creatures the Irish and Welsh usually think of as 'the little people.'

"To add to this feeling of magic among us, the mushroom, you see, has always meant something special, because we have known since time beyond recall that these strange, sometimes very beautiful growths have amazing powers. Every Mycetian family has always had its own kind of mushroom as a personal crest or sign, just as human families have their own coats of arms.

"But instead of having the coat of arms mounted upon a shield, each of our families has always had a small round stone amulet, called a Mushroom Stone, handed down from generation to generation through the youngest son. On it is carved the family mushroom, along with many other curious signs having

40

meaning only to that particular family. Here is mine." And out of an inner pocket Mr. Bass drew forth a small, circular object.

It was about an inch and a half across, flat on the bottom and rounded on the top like a mushroom head. It was gray, smooth and timeworn, and on the domed side had deep lines cut into it which crossed at the center so that the dome was divided into pie-shaped wedges. And on each of these wedges was a different, finely carved, intricate little sign, one of which was plainly a mushroom.

David stared at it, fascinated, and with a faint shock of recognition. Where — *where* had he seen signs like that before? He could not remember for the life of him, and now Tyco was continuing:

"These little amulets turn up, every once in a while, in the soil of Wales, with the carvings so badly worn that it is impossible for any of us to know what families once owned them. But when a human being finds one, he says it is magic and uses it as a charm.

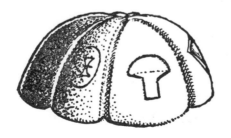

And if gypsies or conjurers find them, they collect them to counter the powers of witchery. They demand a fee in silver and then hide one of them near the place of human trouble. But we always get them back when we can, and the Mycetian League keeps them —"

"The Mycetian League!" exclaimed David. "What's that, Mr. Bass? It sounds like secret meetings and all sorts of plans being hatched at night off in the woods somewhere —"

"Or in a mountain hideaway, maybe," Chuck put in.

"It *was* like that, centuries ago. You see," said Mr. Bass, looking off as though he were gazing down the long, shadowy tunnel of time, "it started as the Mycetian League in the fifth century A.D. at the time of Merlin and of Uther Pendragon, the father of Arthur, King of the Britons. Of course, for thousands of years before that, there had been a powerful central group, but only in Merlin's time was it given this name. And it had its rituals and secret meeting places and traditions which were strengthened because the Mycetians were great fighters and helped Arthur to hold Wales against the invading Saxons."

"And you say there is still this League, Mr. Bass?" asked Chuck eagerly.

"Oh, yes — in Wales, and always it has had just

thirteen specially chosen members. Thirteen, you know, is a good number, a fortunate number among my people."

"Are you a member of the League, Mr. Bass?" asked David, hoping with all his heart that Mr. Bass was, and somehow being certain of it.

Tyco nodded, smiling at him.

"Yes, David, someone in my family has always belonged to it, and this is a very great privilege — a supreme honor, because the League keeps in touch with Mycetians all over the world. It helps them in trouble and judges whenever any wrong has been done to them or by them. The League is our court of law."

"And so you know all the secret rituals and traditions and meeting places?"

Again Tyco nodded, and at this, Austin Shellworthy reached out and put his hand on Mr. Bass's arm in the greatest excitement.

"Tyco, as you're a member of the League, would you draw a map for me showing exactly where this burying ground of the Mycetians is?"

"But, Austin, no member of the League, or any Mycetian, has the right to tell you, who are a human. And even if I drew you a map, you would find it strangely difficult to follow. Oddly enough, you must be *shown* the way —"

At this, Austin Shellworthy's eyes widened in disbelief.

"But it must be on a certain spot on earth!" he protested.

"Yes, as a matter of fact it is near Llanbedr, as you gathered from the rune. But it would do you no good to know this. Have you ever, in your dreams, known perfectly well where a certain street or house was and struggled and struggled to find it and yet felt that it continually eluded you? It would be like that —"

Dr. Shellworthy unfolded his long legs and got down from the stool. He put a hand on each of Tyco's arms and shook him in his earnestness.

"You sound as if you believe in magic —!" And then, as he found himself lifting little Mr. Bass right up in the air, he let out a gasp of stifled amazement. "Why, Tyco, you must not weigh anything! A child of seven could lift you —"

"Yes, Austin, that is the way we Mycetians are built — light as birds. Try again."

Now Dr. Shellworthy gave Mr. Bass a good, firm heft, whereupon Tyco shot up into the air with such suddenness that Dr. Shellworthy let out another gasp of horrified amazement.

But Mr. Bass only laughed. "The reason those bones the boys found are rather heavy is because

44

they've absorbed certain elements during the passing millenniums. And of course this is why they do not glow as brightly as they would otherwise. But as for

45

our birdlike lightness when we are alive, I've often wondered if it might not have something to do with our compressibility."

"Your *what?*" exclaimed Austin Shellworthy.

"Take a good hold of me, Austin, and see what happens. You're a fairly strong man, I should say."

Dr. Shellworthy's expression seemed almost to mean, David saw with delight, that he practically expected Tyco to disappear at any moment (oh, what would he say, David wondered with inner laughter, if he knew that Mr. Bass could?) But he put out his arms, closed them around Tyco's slight body as tightly as he could, and locked his fingers firmly together. Yet in a breath Tyco had somehow slipped free and stood some little distance away, smiling at his friend with that bright glance of his.

This last demonstration of the difference, the unique and mysterious abilities of the Mycetians, seemed too much for Dr. Shellworthy. He sat down on Tyco's stool and struck his hand against his head as though to bring himself back to reality.

"Tyco," he said, "what with one thing and another, I simply do not know what to think. How many years we have been friends — and how little I have really known about you! All I can do is to go home now and put all this down on paper, together with whatever facts I can get from a study of the bones. Then perhaps I shall have the courage to break the news to the rest of the Department of Anthropology." Here, however, he groaned. "You know," he went on, and once more he got up and began pacing with that air of his rather like a tall, kindly and worried crane, as David's mother had once put it, "you know, I don't see how we're to keep this discovery to ourselves. And if it gets into the newspapers and is broadcast over the radio and on television before we've had a chance to do more testing and a lot of digging to see what else we can find, we'll have dozens of people — scientists and amateur anthropologists — pouring in on us and asking questions and offering help, and then we're done for! It'll be awful — simply awful!"

"But it *won't* get into the papers, Dr. Shellworthy," said David firmly. "Because we won't tell anyone, will we, Chuck? None of us'll say a word. And that's a promise."

CHAPTER 7

"It Must Be the World Arrived"

THE fine, sparkling-clear weather, which had shone like a blessing on the Peninsula ever since that out-of-season storm, continued to hold, and David wakened early to a patch of deep-blue sky gleaming through the branches of Monterey pine just outside his window. Squirrels sent their busy, chattering calls from one treetop to another, and a redheaded woodpecker riveted for insects with that terrible energy and persistence which only woodpeckers can work up. David sometimes wondered if they ever got headaches.

Then, all at once, there was complete silence outside and he heard his mother, from the direction of the kitchen, uttering exclamations of shocked surprise. He listened, holding his breath, but he could not make out her words. It was her tone that had caught his ear.

Like a shot he was out of bed and running for the kitchen.

48

"What is it, Mom?" he called. "What's the matter?"

There at the breakfast table, which was in a corner of the big sunny room where two wide windows joined to give a view out over the sea, were his mother and father with the morning paper. Mrs. Topman, the coffeepot in her hand, was bending over Dr. Topman, who was sitting down with the paper spread in front of him. As David came in, she looked up.

"David!" she said. "How could it possibly have gotten out?"

He swallowed, and at the same time felt a horrible sinking in the pit of his stomach.

"Gotten out?" he repeated faintly. "What's gotten out?"

"Come here and look," was all she was able to answer.

David came and looked. And there, right across the top of the front page, were three lines of enormous black type: *HALF-MILLION-YEAR-OLD HUMAN REMAINS FOUND HERE!*

A sliver of ice shot up David's spine and the sinking in his stomach seemed to condense into something so large and heavy and solid that he had to sit down.

"Oh, golly," he whispered in a sick voice, "oh golly,

49

what'll Mr. Bass say?" What little was left of his summer tan faded right away.

"What will he *say!*" cried Mrs. Topman. "But, David, *he* is the one who spoke to the newspaper reporter, it says here! Though of course only because the reporter already knew, somehow, and came to Mr. Bass to get more information."

David pulled the paper toward him and, horrified yet fascinated, his eyes traveled down from the head-line and studied that dreadful first page.

"But I didn't tell, Mom and Dad — honestly I didn't. And neither did Chuck. I *know* he didn't."

"We were quite sure of that, David," his father reassured him. But he seemed quite concerned.

There was a picture of Mr. Bass and, underneath it, a column telling what a famous astronomer and inventor and artist he was. Then there was an interview with him by the writer of the column, who was, according to the by-line, one Tim Wilkins.

Hastily David ran his finger down the lines of type hunting for his and Chuck's names; and there they were as the discoverers of the half-million-year-old human remains. But there was not a word about Dr. Shellworthy nor about the bones being found on his property. And why wasn't there? David wondered at once. Because if the reporter had gotten out of Mr. Bass *who* found the bones, why hadn't he gotten

the information about *where* they had been found? Tim Wilkins would be wild to know that!

At the bottom of the column it said to turn to an inside page. And when David turned over, he saw a big chart showing the evolution of man, with pictures of what he may have looked like at various stages. Going back from the present, it showed that a man we call Cro-Magnon man lived between 25,000 and 50,000 years ago. Neanderthal man, the chart said, came into existence somewhere between 50,000 and 300,000 years ago, and Heidelberg man around 300,000 years ago. Opposite the 500,000-year line were Java ape-man and Peking man. And in a heavily outlined space at this point was a black-lettered question: Does Pacific Grove man belong here also?

As he stared at those words, David felt his head swim. Then he looked to where it explained that ancient human remains are usually named after the place where they are found.

"Pacific Grove man," he breathed. "That little Mycetian! And Chuck and I found him!"

"But what I don't understand," said Mrs. Topman, "is why Mr. Bass, when Tim Wilkins interviewed him, had to tell all this."

"Well, you notice," pointed out Dr. Topman, "that Mr. Bass doesn't really tell anything at all that he doesn't have to. He simply said 'Yes,' to some questions and 'No,' to others. He couldn't fib."

"But why doesn't it say who gave the secret away?" went on Mrs. Topman. "Only four people knew, and if Chuck or David didn't tell, and Mr. Bass didn't, then that leaves Dr. Shellworthy and surely he wouldn't —"

"And *why* isn't there anything about Dr. Shellworthy or about the bones glowing in the dark?" puzzled David. "I'm going to phone Mr. Bass — that's what I'm going to do," he decided suddenly, jumping up.

In the hall he dialed Tyco's number, and while the line buzzed, he heard the radio go on in the kitchen so that he was reminded at once that maybe this was the next thing they'd have to face: their discovery being broadcast everywhere, up and down the whole Pacific Coast, over the entire nation sooner or later, and after that, the phone probably ringing all day long, and people coming.

Then there it was, Mr. Bass's courteous, rather flutelike, "Tyco Bass speaking —"

"Mr. Bass," and how David's heart beat, even though he was positive he hadn't said a word to anybody, "we just got the paper —" He was terribly embarrassed to hear how his voice wobbled.

"Ah, yes, David, it's unfortunate, isn't it?" came

the calm, unruffled reply. "However, don't feel badly. As Austin Shellworthy said to me just before he left last night, 'The most unlooked-for things can happen —' and, it has turned out, the most unlooked-for thing *did* happen!"

"You mean somebody came in on Dr. Shellworthy in his office when he was working on the bones?"

"No, David. I mean that a small boy by the name of Jimmy Chipping, my little next-door neighbor, happened to be hiding in the bushes when you and Chuck went home last night — talking, no doubt, in your excitement, about the bones and how old I said they were. It is all perfectly understandable, your excitement and Jimmy's wanting everybody to know."

David's face went hot with mingled fury and guilt.

"You mean Jimmy Chipping went and —"

"But you mustn't be angry with him, David! He's so proud he knows you, and he had no idea it was a secret, so that I hadn't the heart to get after him. All the same," finished Tyco, "I imagine we're in for it."

There was a short pause, and then:

"Mr. Bass, it really is Chuck's and my fault after all, isn't it?" David was certain he'd never been so unhappy in his whole life.

"But how could you possibly have guessed," came

Tyco's comforting voice, "that Jimmy would be hiding in the bushes waiting to jump out on you? And you were both talking so hard, he said, and saying such surprising things, and then you hopped on your bikes and rode away so fast, he just stayed where he was and didn't say a word.

"Anyway, David, we must just accept what has happened, and deal with events as they come along. Dr. Shellworthy doesn't come into it for the present, thank goodness, because luckily you didn't mention him within Jimmy's hearing, nor where you'd found the bones — and, oh, wouldn't Tim Wilkins have given his shirt to know. He'll be on your trail today —"

"We won't say a word, Mr. Bass —"

"No, because Austin *must* have a chance to get one of those high, steel-link fences put up around his entire property. He's having the work started this morning."

"Mr. Bass, just who did Jimmy Chipping tell?"

"Oh, it was a friend of the family's, a young fellow who works at the radio station," returned Tyco. "But he laughed, thinking of course that such a preposterous story was simply a small boy's imagining, something he'd like to have happen. But then this young fellow happened to say something to Tim Wilkins over at the paper late last night, and that

55

was when Tim got busy. He called me at about one this morning —

"There! Knocking at the door already. I'm afraid it must be the world arrived, by the sound — probably the TV people. Good-by, David, and when they get to you and your parents, remember — *hold firm!*"

Which David had to do.

For no sooner had he hung up, than the front doorbell rang, and it was a young man who announced himself as Tim Wilkins.

"I'm a little late, David," he said, upon learning that this *was* David, "but I wonder if I might have a few words with you. I'd have been around about three this morning, but the only way I could get my story from Tyco Bass on your discovery was to make him a promise I'd wait. He said he wanted you and Chuck to have your sleep."

CHAPTER 8

A Disappearance

THAT had been on the morning of Tuesday, September 21.

It was now six-thirty in the evening, seven days later on September 28, precisely half an hour before Tyco was to leave for the Galaxy M 81 in Ursa Major.

Those seven days had been just as hectic as Dr. Shellworthy had predicted they would be. "Pacific Grove man" was on everyone's lips. Dr. Shellworthy, the minute that steel-link fence had been put up around his property, told just where the discovery had been made. And every day there was a crowd outside the fence asking questions, offering suggestions, and begging to be let in and help dig. Chuck and David were so bombarded with questions at school, and their class so disrupted, that Miss Pilchard, their teacher, finally lost patience entirely and would not permit the subject to be mentioned.

"I think David and I ought to stay out of school for a while, don't you, Miss Pilchard?" Chuck had suggested hopefully. But she didn't seem to think this extreme measure would be necessary.

The worst part was, what with phones ringing, telegrams and even cablegrams arriving, mail piling up, neighbors dropping in at all hours to ask both foolish and sensible questions and getting under foot generally, famous archaeologists and anthropologists arriving from all over, and newspaper reporters asking for interviews, Mr. Bass had not been able to get ahead with his work of overhauling the space ship for a single minute. Therefore, even if Ta had sent word for the boys to come at once, they couldn't have taken off.

Finally, with the time for Mr. Bass's departure drawing near, Mrs. Topman had stayed on guard the last two days at Number 5 to fend off visitors and to answer the phone until David and Chuck could come by after school to relieve her.

At last, just in time, Mr. Bass finished taking the workings of the space ship entirely apart and putting them all back together again. Besides overhauling the rocket motor, he had rechecked every delicate little wire, had gone over each instrument and its connections including the auto-reversatron, and had double-checked the fuel jets. However, the fluid resinoid silicon sealer that Mr. Bass had concocted as a protective coating against cosmic and solar rays for

58

the inside and outside of the ship had not quite ripened yet. And of course the fuel tanks containing the fuel with Tyco's special atomic tritetramethylbenzacarbonethylene in it which could blow a mountain to smithereens — ten mountains, in fact — were still piled up in the cave down on Cap'n Tom's beach. These would have to be slipped into place at the last minute.

Now Tyco stood back and surveyed the ship, just about ready to depart on its journey to Basidium the minute Ta said, "Come!"

"He's just *got* to tell us it's all right, Mr. Bass," David was saying. "Even if Ta says he'll give us only a few pieces of Brumblium, that would allow Mr. Brumblydge to go ahead with his Brumblitron for a while anyway. Everything he wants to do — even his Theory of the Universe — depends on his getting that Brumblium, doesn't it, because of all the experiments he wants to make?"

"It does, indeed, David," agreed Tyco, and now he picked up from his workbench a sheet of paper which looked to David like a hastily scribbled message. " '— a run of extremely bad luck lately,' " David thought he heard Mr. Bass murmur. Then Mr. Bass shook his head in a puzzled fashion and folded the paper, while a multitude of ideas seemed to be

darting back and forth in his head. "Ah, but it doesn't make sense — it just doesn't make sense at all — not any way you look at it," he said softly.

"Is that a note you want us to give somebody, Mr. Bass?"

60

"No, David. Prewytt wrote me this the morning he left to go back to San Julian."

David and Chuck studied Mr. Bass's face attentively.

"Are you still feeling uneasy?" Chuck wanted to know.

"Yes — precisely as I felt the day before you found the bones, which was also the day before Prewytt returned to San Julian. I remember it was then that I first became aware of this feeling of mine, this restless foreboding. That was the night of the storm." Now Tyco put his hands lightly for a moment on Chuck's and David's shoulders. "I have been concerned about Prewytt, you know — in fact, so much so that three times I have flitted up to San Julian to have a little talk with him."

"You *have*?" cried the boys together, trying their best to picture Mr. Bass appearing and disappearing as he thought himself from Pacific Grove to San Julian and back again.

"Yes, and twice he did not even recognize me in the depths of his fever, and the last time, about an hour ago, he was fast asleep and I hadn't the heart to awaken him." Mr. Bass folded Prewytt's note and put it away in a drawer. "Well, now, boys, one last thing before I go — you *must* keep your heads at the meeting tonight."

"You mean, then," asked David, "that you think we'll *need* to?"

What had happened was this. A week or so before the discovery of Pacific Grove man, Dr. Shellworthy had promised the Society of Young Astronomers and Students of Space Travel (which David and Chuck had started and which met once a month) that he would be happy to give them a talk on What Intelligent Beings of Other Planets May Look Like. But Dr. Shellworthy was by this time in no shape to give a talk, and had wanted very much to beg off.

Then Chuck and David had a brilliant idea.

"Dr. Shellworthy, Dave and I have been thinking — well, my Gramp put in a thought, too — and it's about the bones. What you want is to find out *if* this whole thing is a hoax or not, and *if* it is — who put the bones in the cliff. Well, I'll bet — that is, Dave 'n' I'll bet — that if you give this talk and then answer questions about it afterwards, the person who did this'll probably be there —"

"— and we think he'll ask plenty of questions," interrupted David, "and they'll be about Pacific Grove man, just so he can laugh to himself over the answers. So maybe, somehow, we can spot who the guilty one is."

Austin Shellworthy was silent for a minute. Then:

"Boys, you're a pair of wonders. And, by heaven, it's worth a try. Now, look — we'll want the news spread all over town as to just what the talk will be about, and that I'll be discussing Pacific Grove man as well. But especially we'll want it advertised that there'll be a question and answer period afterwards —"

"So Dave and I'll get busy right away making big signs," broke in Chuck eagerly, "and we'll go around on our bikes real early tomorrow morning before school and nail 'em up everywhere."

Which they had done. The Young Astronomers were to meet at seven-thirty tonight in the library of SAGA Hall (Society of Anthropologists, Geologists and Archaeologists), and Dr. Shellworthy had his talk all ready.

"Mr. Bass," said David, "would you tell us that rune about the bones once more?"

Mr. Bass said it over slowly so that David and Chuck would know it forever:

"Remember the ancient words of Wyrd,
Carved at Llanbedr by a hand afeard —
That blackest misfortune shall follow him hard
Who robs our graves near the mountain's guard.

And he, thus cursed, must return our bones,
Who would free himself of the rune of the stones."

"Well, then," said David thoughtfully, "if the Mycetian bones *don't* belong in the cliff — I mean, if some little Mycetian *didn't* die there half a million years ago — and if someone who is alive now took the bones away from Wales and buried them here for some reason or other, why, he's in bad trouble, isn't he?"

Mr. Bass shook his head.

"I don't know, David. After all, it's only an old rune. But it might be well if that person returned them to the graveyard at the top of the Roman Steps near Llanbedr in Wales just as quickly as possible."

Now David could tell by the way Mr. Bass was tidying up the last few stray odds and ends on his workbench that he was ready to go. The small round clock said two minutes of seven, and that vibrant current of happiness and excitement was about to be cut once more, the current both he and Chuck felt so intensely between themselves and Mr. Bass whenever they were together, or even if they were just in the house somewhere and he was working in another room. They would not feel it again, perhaps, for a long, long time.

"Mr. Bass," said Chuck in rather an odd voice,

"could we — that is — could David and I — watch you disappear?" He looked slightly embarrassed, as if he thought Mr. Bass might think this disappearing business was somehow private.

Mr. Bass laid a slender, faintly greenish finger alongside his nose and chuckled.

"Why, of course you may, Chuck. That is, if it won't upset you or make you feel peculiar. After all, it is rather an unusual thing for a person to do, isn't it, and not something you might witness just any day."

"I think we'd like to, Mr. Bass," said David seriously. "Except that we hate like the dickens to see you go. Please come back soon."

"As soon as I can, David — that I promise you. How I shall miss you both! Now" — he held out his hands and the boys grasped them — "remember to keep calm tonight and through all the crises and decisions that will no doubt follow in the days to come. I wish I could be here, but I know that I can trust you. There is to be a meeting of the Mycetian League in two weeks, and I just may be able to attend. Of course it will be in Wales, but if you are having great difficulty I might manage to drop by here for an hour or two. We shall see. Good-by, my friends —"

His hands slipped from theirs as though his flesh

were nothing but a breath of wind. He smiled; his large, dark-brown eyes sparkled. In the flash of an instant, David took in for the last time his old gray gardening coat, his elastic-sided boots, his hands outheld with their long fingers, and his small, kindly face beneath the great, domed head with its few wisps of hair.

Then he was gone. Where had been the gardening coat and elastic-sided boots was nothing. The air seemed to have stirred a little, but in the cellar work-room David and Chuck were quite alone.

CHAPTER 9

Up at Mrs. Cuttle's

Precisely on the dot of seven, at the very split second in which Mr. Bass was thinking himself back to his new home in a solar system in the Galaxy M 81 in Ursa Major, Prewytt woke from sleep with a start.

"Wrong!" he cried aloud, and rose right up from his pillow, staring at the wall beyond the foot of his bed. "*Wrong!*" And it was his fossil-dating process he meant, his process that he'd actually boasted of, just a bit cockily, to Austin Shellworthy when Austin had asked, "And what can your invention do for me, an anthropologist, Prewytt?"

Boasted, yes, Prewytt remembered. Because the tests he'd made had appeared to prove his dating process so beautifully! All the same, he must not have been certain, not deep-down certain. For his mind had been at work even during his fever and later while he slept, and now he knew as clear as clear could be that he'd made an error, and that that

67

error would multiply with the testing of increasingly older fossils.

Prewytt sat up, turned on the lamp, and took a pencil and some three-by-five white cards from the little table at the side of his bed. Then he began going over his process step by step, writing out exceedingly neat equations and checking them again and again.

When he had finished, it was quite plain to him that he had indeed made one tiny error. He stared at the cards.

"But then, in that case," he whispered, "in *that* case — oh, but it doesn't seem possible! Why — why, then — I must go back to Pacific Grove at once!"

But at this moment Mrs. Lilly Cuttle, a quick, bright-eyed little woman, put her head in at Prewytt's bedroom door.

"Well, hel-lo-o there, Mr. Brumblydge," she sang out in a high, carrying voice, seeing him awake and sitting up with the lamp on. "So we're feeling much, much better! How would our patient like some nice, hot chicken broth I made myself, and some newspapers to read? I brought them along with me — just in case." She looked really pleased as she came over to him, but Prewytt did not even seem to notice her. "Why, Mr. Brumblydge," she said, studying his expression, "is there anything wrong? You look as if someone had hit you."

"Not someone, Mrs. Cuttle," he replied quietly, "something." Then he leaned forward as though to throw off the blankets. "And I must get up and go this very minute —" but suddenly he cocked his head. "What was that?"

Mrs. Cuttle cocked *her* head.

"Rain!" she exclaimed. "Rain again! Now, if that isn't the most irritating thing, and just when I was looking forward to my bridge club this evening. It's like a week or two ago — another one of those freak storms — and just as sudden. Oh, it's positively uncanny, as if somebody up there'd suddenly taken it into his head to turn over a million washtubs. There now, listen to it! Why, it's *pouring!*"

Rain lashed and beat against the windows, washing down in solid sheets. Then the lamp dimmed for an instant when a tongue of lightning shot out far overhead from among swollen clouds. A moment later — "*POM!*" and a giant cannon ball of thunder, sounding as if it had made a direct hit on the observatory, bellowed its way down the mountain.

"Oh," said Mrs. Cuttle, shivering and looking up, "that settles it. In I stay. Here are your papers, Mr. Brumblydge. Some of 'em are a little old, but that doesn't matter seeing as how you have so much to catch up on. Now, you just stay here nice and cozy and I'll have your broth up in two ticks."

Away she went. But Mr. Brumblydge, still cogitating upon what that one small, enormously important error in his dating process could mean, drew the top newspaper toward him. Idly he passed an eye over the headlines, and then, as if hypnotized, his appalled and unbelieving gaze fixed itself upon those big black letters:

HALF-MILLION-YEAR-OLD PACIFIC GROVE MAN SPLITS SCIENTISTS!

they shouted. Prewytt's hand holding the newspaper began to tremble and his eyes flashed down first one column and then another.

Four days ago [read Prewytt] the incredible discovery of the two boys, David Topman and Chuck Masterson of Pacific Grove, California, was made known to the public. Since then, the world of science has been more sharply divided over those three pieces of bone than it ever was over the great Piltdown Hoax.

Last night the fluorine testing of the bones was completed. Because of its results and the results of other tests, it is now accepted that so-called Pacific Grove man is actually around 500,000 years old. So far, no remains of ancient man have been found on either the North American or the South American

Continent which can be dated at older than 50,000 years.

"I believe," says Dr. Ambrose Mellander Bullen, famous for the fact that he is so often at odds with his fellow scientists, "that this discovery will prove the truth of what I have been saying for so long. Very ancient man *did* come across the Bering Straits and down through Alaska into the Americas thousands and thousands of years before most anthropologists have thought it likely.

"I believe that this find is *not* a hoax. I believe that the bones, two of which were washed out by the heavy rains, do actually belong in the cliff on Dr. Austin Shellworthy's property. For one thing, it has been proved by the strata of the cliff that this spot was in times past the fill-in of an ancient cave. Here, Pacific Grove man could well have lived half a million years ago."

Half a million years ago! Prewytt's eyes, unable to rest, darted wildly, unbelievingly, from column to column, from paragraph to paragraph.

. . . The noted French archaeologist, Jean de la Place, flew over from France yesterday, to be followed today by Professors Lyle Buford Pippin and N. Treford-Oldenstern from London. Josuah P. Dingley, an anthropologist from Boston, Massachusetts, is in sharp disagreement with Tyco Bass, the famous astronomer. Bass has said that the bones are those of an ancient Mycetian, or spore person.

72

But Dingley states that this is simply ridiculous, for the very good reason that there is no such race as the Mushroom People. He also states that he has never heard of Mycetians.

Prewytt passed a shaking hand across his perspiring forehead and read on further down:

. . . What is most mysterious, perhaps, is the fact that the bones glow in the dark. According to Dr. Shellworthy, this glow seems to resemble that of some types of mushrooms that have their own built-in lighting systems.

One of the most brilliant glowers, he says, is the honey mushroom. When it is broken open in the daylight, the whole inside seems to be a mass of gray cobwebs, but in the dark the cobwebs shine a brilliant blue. The bones of Pacific Grove man give off a luminous, pale, greenish-silver glow. If they *are* the bones of a spore person, Shellworthy states, then there may be some similar process at work because, as everyone knows, mushrooms are spore-bearing plants.

Prewytt lifted his head as if for air, then returned to his reading.

The most unfortunate person in the whole affair [his wretched eye hit upon next] is Dr. Shellworthy himself. He has had to have several hundred feet of steel-link fence put up around his entire property at great expense, as his lot is an extremely large one. Furthermore, he says that neither he nor his wife have had a moment's peace since the discovery was first announced.

"*Oh!*" cried Prewytt aloud, and a groan escaped him as he struck his fist against his head. He flung the paper away, looked wildly about his bedroom as though trying to gather his wits, then pushed back the covers and got out of bed.

For a second or two he wavered. But, shivering and shuddering, he made his way to the closet and got out a suit and a pair of shoes. Next he burrowed in his dresser drawer for clean underthings, socks, and a shirt and bow tie. Then, listening meanwhile to the dreadful torrent beating against the side of the house, he stuffed his unwilling legs into his trousers, thought of shaving, shook his head despairingly, fumbled into a jacket, got his hat, raincoat and umbrella, and made his way downstairs.

Now he stood bracing himself to step out into the merciless downpour. But in that moment there came to him some lines of verse about Wyrd that he'd known when he was young. Without warning they came, in the clear, unmistakable voice of his Aunt Matilda Brumblydge from the old days in Wales:

Remember the ancient words of Wyrd,
Carved at Llanbedr by a hand afeard —
That blackest misfortune shall follow him hard

74

Who robs our graves near the mountain's guard.
And he, thus cursed, must return our bones,
Who would free himself of the rune of the stones.

A moment later, the door of Mrs. Cuttle's boardinghouse opened and clapped-to behind him. And Mrs. Cuttle, scraping burned toast in the kitchen, did not even hear.

CHAPTER 10

A Disastrous Meeting

PROBABLY no one should have been in the least surprised at the way the meeting of Young Astronomers and Students of Space Travel turned out. For it began badly despite Chuck and David's being so pleased about the attendance.

Chuck thought it a wonderful piece of luck that they had not been able to get the high school auditorium, and that the whole crowd of Young Astronomers, their families, and visiting scientists had to pack themselves into the library of SAGA Hall. This was a well-lighted, beautiful room with books all around the walls, and everybody was drawn cozily together instead of being lost in the cold, large dimensions of the auditorium.

"— and besides, *this* way," Chuck hissed into David's ear, "we can keep a *much* better eye out for the culprit —"

"— if there is one," finished David, but he sounded much more sensible than he wanted to be.

76

The boys gazed around in pride. The reading tables had been taken out, and, at twenty-five minutes after seven, every seat was full, with more people pushing in with folding chairs. Even the dignitaries had come! There was neat, dark little Dr. Jean de la Place next to pale, prim, wiry Josuah P. Dingley. He was looking somewhat aloof and disdainful; for if there was one thing he did not believe in, it was intelligent life on other planets. Next to him was the great Dr. Ambrose Mellander Bullen (great in every respect: width, height, and weight as well as ability, and taking up space enough for two), along with the Londoners Lyle Buford Pippin and N. Treford-Oldenstern. These gentlemen sat in a solid row of learning.

But no sooner had everyone gotten settled and quiet, with Dr. Shellworthy up on the platform with a blackboard, plenty of chalk, and easels holding all sorts of big charts and diagrams, than Dr. Ambrose Mellander Bullen began blowing out clouds of horribly strong cigar smoke.

"Pheeee-*yew!*" shouted Chuck, holding his nose and turning around to glare indignantly at Dr. Bullen.

"Oh, my, I really don't think I can stand —" cried Annabelle Topman. At this, other exclamations of protest rose from various persons around the cigar, quite drowning out Dr. Shellworthy.

"Well, now, I wonder," he began anxiously, waving a piece of chalk, "if perhaps the windows could be —"

But at this point the real trouble began. For Dr. Bullen arose and, in a deep, commanding voice, made a motion that the "Outer Space" part of the program (here he waved his cigar as though scornfully dismissing it) be skipped entirely and the whole meeting given over to "Pacific Grove man." This motion was seconded at once by little Dr. Dingley, but it was quickly and sternly voted down by all the Young Astronomers and Students of Space Travel. What was more, Dr. Bullen was told in sharp tones by an outspoken lady that there was a distinct sign on the wall saying that smoking was not allowed in the library. Whereupon Dr. Bullen put out his cigar, but his face turned a dark, purplish red.

Now the meeting got under way again, but by this time poor Dr. Shellworthy, who was really a very shy man and quite sensitive, seemed to be somewhat shaken by this bad beginning. He did the best he could, but he kept looking at Dingley and Bullen, who were staring coldly at him, and he hurried with his talk whether he meant to or not.

Of course Chuck and David noticed this. And what with the smelly cigar smoke still hanging in a nauseous cloud in the air, doors and windows being opened so that rain-damp drafts scuttled in around everyone's legs, people muttering and murmuring, and their perfectly good meeting being absolutely ruined, the boys slowly got madder and madder. So that when the really disastrous part of the evening exploded without warning, they were ready for it.

The first thing that happened after Dr. Shellworthy finished was that a woman demanded to know if it was possible some respected and well-known scientist could have planted the bones there, just as had happened in the Piltdown Hoax.

"Maybe it was *him* — Shellworthy —" sniggered a big, overgrown boy up front, but he said it much too loudly.

Then what an uproar there was from Dr. Shellworthy's students, who all seemed to be seated in the first two rows! At the same time Chuck and David leaped up and joined in.

"Quiet, Chuck!" ordered Cap'n Tom, and out came his big hand on Chuck's shoulder. But it was too late. At this moment, a boy who had been nagging Chuck and David at school all during the past week about their peculiar little friend, Tyco Mushroom Bass, with the funny clothes and the big head, now turned around and grinned at them, his eyes all squinted up.

"Where is he?" he yelled. "Where's Mr. Tyco Bass? He's not here! I bet he invented that lighting-up business just before he stuck the bones in the cliff himself — !"

In a flash, Chuck, stocky and strong as a young bullock, was on him. People got out of the way, chairs were knocked over, and another boy made a grab for David, who hit back furiously (he really didn't like to fight, but he'd have fought anybody over Mr. Bass). And before anyone could tell just how it had all happened, there was a whole knot of tangled, flailing arms and legs which seemed to belong to many more than four boys.

Now voices were raised from the row of learning and Dr. Bullen's voice boomed forth:

". . . but I wish to retain above all an open mind, I tell you — it is what I have been trying to do from the beginning —"

"And *I* say it is so open," piped up little Dingley heatedly, "that the wind is blowing through it!"

After that, nobody really knew what happened, except that members of the Young Astronomers and Students of Space Travel, who were all on Mr. Bass's and Dr. Shellworthy's side, seemed to be fighting the nonmembers who were not. And what with grown-ups trying to separate them, and Dr. Bullen roaring at Dr. Dingley, and Dr. Shellworthy banging with his gavel on the table, and Cap'n Tom and Dr. Topman trying to get hold of Chuck and David, who were the most enraged boys present, the meeting broke up in chaos.

But there was worse trouble to come.

For now, as David glanced up from his pummeling, he saw Dr. Shellworthy suddenly cease his gavel banging with a look of mingled amazement, anxiety, and deep concern. David turned to where Dr. Shellworthy was staring and there — there at the door of the library — beheld Prewytt Brumblydge.

But never, as long as David had known him, had he beheld *such* a Prewytt Brumblydge!

It was not just his appearance. True, he looked as if he had slept in his clothes for weeks, but David had seen him once only a few hours after he had almost drowned. No, this was terribly different. It was his expression.

He looked wild — haunted — desperate. His eyes glittered. His face was deathly pale, and yet there was a spot of greenish-yellow in each cheek. His mouth was open as if he found it hard to breathe. Now he leaned against the door and raised an arm as though to quell the rioting, and something between a groan and a dreadful, rough bark, barely audible among all the scuffling and trampling, escaped him. Now Dr. Shellworthy raised *his* voice, calling out a stern command for order, and a murmurous silence fell.

"Please!" croaked Prewytt as though his throat were sandpaper, or as if he were almost too sick to speak. And everyone turned, their eyes widening as though they were confronted by a ghost. "Please — I have something to say. There is no need — no need to argue and fight. Dr. Shellworthy is not guilty. Tyco Bass is not guilty. These are honorable men who have been hoodwinked. For there is no Pacific Grove man. The bones do not belong in the cliff. And I should know — because I put them there —"

His hoarse voice broke off, and an almost unbelieving gasp rose from that roomful of people.

"Prewytt Brumblydge!" broke from the lips of those who knew him, or who had heard of the difficult and important work he was doing.

"Who is he? Who is he?" cried others who did not know of him, rising up in their seats to have a good look.

"Quick, Tom, quick!" cried Dr. Topman to Cap'n Tom, and in another moment they were pushing their way through the close-packed aisles. Fortunately — how very fortunately! — they got the poor, crumpled Prewytt out into the hall just before the whole press of people rose up and began streaming after them.

From there, having gotten him downstairs and into the Topmans' station wagon, they whisked him

83

home and put him into the spare bedroom at once. And fifteen minutes later, when Mrs. Topman and Dr. Shellworthy came in with the boys, Prewytt was running a temperature of 104 and babbling nonsense about being blown up and hurled into ravines and about thunderstorms and running out of gasoline, and about the burial ground at Llanbedr and about someone by the name of Morgan Caerwen.

Later, much later that night, after Dr. Topman had Prewytt quieted down, they all gathered in the living room.

"Oh, I can scarcely believe it," said Mrs. Topman in a low voice, "that Mr. Brumblydge should have done it! But what an incredible coincidence that he should have buried the bones in a cliff in your garden, Austin, and that the boys should have started hunting just *there* for something for the museum."

At this, David stared at her in amazement.

"A *coincidence*, Mom!" he exclaimed. "Well, you just don't understand anything. Look, the rune says:

"*Remember the ancient words of Wyrd . . .*
That blackest misfortune shall follow him
    hard
Who robs our graves near the mountain's
    guard. . . .*"

84

"Don't you see? *If* Mr. Brumblydge stole those bones from the foot of the mountain in Llanbedr — why, then, it wasn't a coincidence at all that we hunted there. And it *wasn't* a coincidence we had a storm in September that washed the bones out of the cliff! And it *wasn't* a coincidence we found them! *That was Wyrd at work!*

PART TWO

A Place of Wonder

CHAPTER 11

David Decides

Now what an uproar shook the world of science! What outcries arose from those who had been taken in. What headlines sprang across the front pages of all the newspapers. Could this, in truth, be called the Great Brumblydge Hoax?

Where had Prewytt Brumblydge got the bones, everyone wanted to know, and when had he put them in the cliff? But above all, what reason would a respected astronomer, who was even now at work on a theory that might well change everyone's ideas about the universe, have for doing such a strange thing? Or for playing such a ridiculous and pointless trick, if trick it was?

Most furious of all, of course, was Dr. Ambrose Mellander Bullen. Just before he got on the plane to go home, he said that if he did not get a certain university position he was considering, the reason would certainly have something to do with Mr. Brumblydge. And it seemed to him very clear that Prewytt Brumblydge was no fit person to hold a responsible job. Could it be possible that Horace Frobisher would consider keeping Mr. Brumblydge on at the San Julian Observatory?

But Dr. Frobisher, the head of the observatory, stuck up for Prewytt when he was asked by newspaper reporters whether he was going to dismiss him. Why, certainly not! he said. And if a few people had been taken in by David's and Chuck's discovery, then that was not Mr. Brumblydge's fault. Perhaps they should have been a great deal smarter than they had turned out to be.

Meanwhile, Prewytt tossed and turned and muttered. He got the bedclothes into an awful tangle and worried himself in his fever until he was sicker than ever, and nothing Dr. Topman could do seemed to help him one whit.

Then, the night before the decision from Basidium was due, Prewytt began singing his old favorite, "Men of Harlech," and then he started reciting poetry, and it sounded unbearably pathetic, wavering out of the spare bedroom.

"*Do diddle di do,*" he piped up faintly, "*poor Jim Jay — got stuck fast in Yesterday — round veered the weathercock — the sun drew in — and stuck was Jim like a rusty pin.*" Silence; then: "*Come tomor-*

*row, the neighbors say — he'll be past crying for —
poor Jim Jay."*

"Oh, I can't stand it," said Mrs. Topman. "Do you suppose that's what's weighing on his mind — that soon he'll be past crying for?"

At this, David motioned to Chuck to come into the living room with him. Chuck had come over after dinner to see how Mr. Brumblydge was getting along, and he had been standing at the foot of the bed watching and listening.

"I'll tell you what we've got to do, Chuck," said David. "We've got to go to Basidium right away, whether we've heard from Ta and Mr. Theo or not, and try to get that Brumblium."

Chuck's eyes widened.

"But, Dave, we can't! Why, even Mr. Bass wouldn't go, after Ta asked him not to, because the Mushroom People have to make up their own minds and not be influenced in any way."

"I know, but just *look* at Mr. Brumblydge. What if he should get worse? Dad can't seem to do anything for him, but if we could just make him know, somehow, that he's going to get his Brumblium, why then I'll bet you he'd take hold and maybe stand a chance of getting better —"

"You mean start off without signaling first."

"No, I think we've got to signal right off, and I

don't think we have any time to waste. I only hope Mr. Brumblydge doesn't — I hope he doesn't —" But David didn't seem to want to finish.

"You mean he might die? Golly, I don't think Wyrd would go that far!"

David looked up at him.

"Well, I do," he said. "I think Wyrd would do anything — just *anything*. And I think we've got to hurry." He turned and went quickly to the door of the bedroom. "Mom and Dad, Chuck and I are going over to Mr. Bass's. We'll be back pretty soon."

Dr. Topman, who was sitting beside Prewytt's bed looking very discouraged, did not even lift his head, and Mrs. Topman nodded as if she had scarcely heard. But she had.

"Don't be gone long, boys, and be careful." She always said that. And she meant with their bikes, crossing the streets where it was shadowy.

So Chuck and David put on their zipper jackets — now in October the nights had turned very cold and sharply clear — and started out.

"Dave, what a night for a take-off!"

Yes, the light of the great, round moon poured down and made a moving, restless path of silver across the dark sea. The whole Monterey Peninsula was bathed in silver and the sky was crowded with stars. Just beyond the Topman's yard at the foot of

the cliff, the ocean breathed and thudded all up and down Cap'n Tom's beach.

How still and deserted it felt in Mr. Bass's garden as the boys hurried along the path under the trees. No warm, welcoming light shone down from the observatory windows to tell them that Mr. Bass was still up there, hard at work. Not a light anywhere — only darkness and silence.

And in that instant when they started up the stairs onto the veranda, David glanced up at the big, cold moon and the question leaped into his head: if they interfered, he and Chuck, and stubbornly insisted on taking things into their own hands to help Mr. Brumblydge, would the vengeful finger of Wyrd remove itself from Prewytt and come to rest on them? Or perhaps now all three of them would be followed hard by blackest misfortune. Would Chuck laugh at such an idea?

In ten minutes they had fitted the Stroboscopic Polarizing Filter to the eyepiece of the telescope and discovered that Basidium was just above the treetops low in the western sky, which meant that it could receive their message. Then David got paper and pencil and in another five minutes they had the message worked out and written down in short and long flashes so that there could not possibly be any mistake:

94

P. Brumblydge sick — in terrible danger — need Brumblium at once — may we come now? C and D.

Then they put Mr. Bass's signaling lantern on the desk, being sure that the hood was drawn tight around it before they turned it up to its fullest power. In order to search the skies for Basidium, they had already, by pressing a button, slid a part of the observatory dome downward so that the night sky glittered above their heads.

"You send, Chuck, while I read out the signals."

Carefully, intently, Chuck moved the lantern hood backward and forward so that the heatless, incredibly powerful beam of silver-green could leap across space to light up Mr. Theo's lantern in the observatory he had built on Basidium.

Anxiously they waited after they had turned their lantern to "receive." Either Mebe or Oru, one or the other of Ta's two little Wise Men, should be on duty to watch for messages. And so seriously did they take their work, so proud were they to have been appointed by Mr. Theo to be watchers and caretakers of his observatory, that never once had they failed to catch a signal.

In a few minutes the answer began coming through. At once Chuck called out and David, who had pencil and paper ready, took down. Twice the message was repeated in a series of long and short flashes, then the lantern went dark again. And when the translation was finished, this proved to be the reply:

Theo and the Great Ta gone to the Hall of the Ancient Ones — do not know when they will return — we cannot speak for them — it is for you to decide but we advise you wait.

MEBE AND ORU

"Oh, Dave!" groaned Chuck in bitter disappointment. "Now what'll we do? But there's nothing we *can* do. Mebe and Oru were right. We've just got to wait."

"The Hall of the Ancient Ones," said David to himself. "That means Mr. Theo and Ta have gone to get advice from Ta's ancestors. Anyhow, the thing is, we'll take off at midnight."

Chuck stared at him as if he'd gone out of his head. "You mean — without permission?"

David nodded, staring at the scrap of paper on which he had written the little Wise Men's message.

"But, Dave, Ta would be furious, and he might never let us come back again, and he'd *never* give us the Brumblium —"

"But I don't think he *will* be furious, Chuck. I know Ta, and I think he'll understand, and I think

96

he'll give us the Brumblium. Anyway, we've got to take a chance. And if you don't want to come, I'll go alone."

Chuck studied David's face for a moment in silence. Then, with quiet determination, "No, you won't, Dave — oh, no, you won't."

CHAPTER 12

The Finger of Wyrd

Two and a half hours later, at a few minutes before midnight, the space ship was down on the beach upended beside the huge rock which the boys always used as a platform. From it they climbed through the doorway of the ship to their seats. David was at the controls and Chuck beside him nearest the door. Now, David thought, for the oxygen urn. If it "pheeps," that means we'll be all right — but if it doesn't —

"Keep your fingers crossed, Dave," and down went Chuck to turn it on.

What a two and a half hours it had been! First of all they couldn't find Cap'n Tom to ask him if Chuck could go, and when David said in desperation that maybe he'd just better go alone, Chuck almost exploded with indignation. He said he'd take *six* lickings when he got back rather than let David go by himself, and he said Dr. and Mrs. Topman were not to feel one bit responsible.

98

Then, next, they'd remembered — just as the boys and Dr. Topman were about to take the space ship on its four-wheeled carrier out of Mr. Bass's cellar to hitch it on to the station wagon — that it hadn't been gone over with the fluid resinoid silicon sealer. And of course they had to put that on, because Mr. Bass had said that it *must* be done before each flight into space. This took a good three quarters of an hour, each working with a big brush just as fast as he could go. And they put a coat on the inside, too, because Mr. Bass had said that was safer.

Then, no sooner had they started home than a policeman stopped them, wanting to know why Dr. Topman had no red taillight for his "trailer." He said this was the first time he'd ever seen a trailer in the shape of a space ship, and he studied it all over from nose to tail in absolute amazement, until David and Chuck thought they would burst into a million pieces with impatience and anxiety. But he had finally let them go when they promised to get a taillight the very next morning.

Last of all, when they had finally got the space ship down onto the beach outside Cap'n Tom's cave, where the fuel tanks were hidden, Dr. Topman hurt his hand quite badly ramming one of them into place. Mrs. Topman, of course, had had to stay with Prewytt, and so Chuck and David had to get the rest of them in all alone, and David was pretty certain the last one had not gone in straight. Would it make a difference?

Now, still shaking from all the worry and hurry they had been through and from hauling and shoving those heavy tanks, David listened tensely for the sound of the oxygen urn. Yes, there it was — "Pheep — pheep — pheep — pheep —" just as steady and nice and sweet as you please, like a little steam engine it sounded, exactly as on their first two journeys. Maybe, after all, the finger of Wyrd was not upon them as he had begun to think, and their flight would be a success.

"We'll be O.K., Dad," he yelled triumphantly, leaning over and sticking his head out of the door. "The oxygen urn 'pheeps' and that means Mr. Bass has every little tiny thing just perfect." Dr. Topman, still nursing his hurt hand, nodded and smiled and then lifted his good hand and waved.

At last the door was closed and bolted tight. The boys strapped themselves in, and then both leaned to peer out of the big plastiglass window above the instrument panel. All up and down the beach the waves curved over, glistening in the flood of moonlight. Dr. Topman moved back — far back from that deadly circle where flame would thunder down from the exhausts.

Then David pressed the starter button. But what was this? There came only a jolting explosion, a rumble of flame — and then silence. Again David pressed the button, and again came the jolting explosion, the brief rumble — and silence.

"Wait a second or two, Dave. Don't keep pressing like that," said Chuck nervously.

"What time is it?"

"Midnight — just exactly midnight."

David felt his heart squeeze up tight until it hurt him, and then it beat furiously. "If you do not leave at midnight pre*cise*ly," he heard Mr. Bass say, and he knew he would never forget those words, "it is dangerously possible that you will not reach Basidium at all." And again, "Time, for you, will be a matter of life and death."

"Oh, Chuck!" he groaned.

Three times more he pressed the button, long and hard, and at last, there it was — the roar that sent a fist pounding right into their stomachs, and Chuck began counting with his eye on the second hand of his watch while the flame from the burning fuel kept bursting down from the exhausts onto the blackening, melting sand.

Dr. Topman stood at the waves' edge with anxious eyes on the space ship sitting in its pool of fire. The boys are in there all alone, he was thinking, and then Chuck in his counting must have come to "ZERO!" — for with an even more stomach-shattering roar the little ship began to rise, slowly at first, slowly, and then up, up against the black sky with its veil of sparkling points, up ever more quickly — until at last a streak of silver sailed away and became a speck, another star, that vanished above the murmuring sea.

CHAPTER 13

Something Impossible

THE atmosphere that blankets earth was thinning from ionosphere to exosphere. A thousand miles high the last molecules of air were left behind, the rocket motor cut itself off, and the ship moved without need of propulsion in absolute darkness and silence. For having once been shot upon its path, and with no atmosphere to impede it, it would sail through the vacuum of space in free fall to its target.

"You all right, Chuck?" David turned groggily to gaze at him.

"I'm all right."

"We started late. How long after midnight was it?"

"Only six seconds."

"Oh, golly — oh, thank goodness! I don't see how six seconds could make a difference." He listened. Yes, it was still going — their oxygen urn — the only sound within the ship. Their talisman, he felt it to be, their good-luck sound, their protection against

104

Wyrd. For Mr. Bass had planned it especially, had twisted the little pipes that permitted just enough oxygen for their breathing in such a way that this cheerful voice could comfort their ears for the whole journey.

Before their eyes, freed of earth's murky blanket that spreads between earth and the endless suns, shone such spangled patterns of light that the enormous shapes of the constellations were almost lost to view. But now their gaze was drawn at once to a blazing star almost directly ahead of their speeding ship, golden-white Altair in the constellation of Aquila, the Eagle. And they saw clearly now, as they had never done before, that it made one point of an enormous triangle whose other two flashing points were blue-white Vega in the Lyre — a little to the northward, with the Ring Nebula nearby — and, higher up, brilliant white Deneb in the Swan. Yes, as Mr. Bass had said, these are three of the most magnificient suns in the heavens.

Still higher in the north and farther back, they saw Alpharetz, which joins Pegasus to the constellation of Andromeda. And within Andromeda they saw at last the Great Nebula in all its glory, that vast sea of one hundred trillion suns which is the brightest of all the nebulae within range of searching eyes on earth, though to them it is only a distant mist.

"I guess we'll never get over being staggered by all this, will we, Chuck? I don't know — it's the first big stupendous view right after we come out of our blackout that's the best. I mean, it makes me feel like pinching myself to be sure this is really me and that all this is really happening."

"Well, let me pinch you, then —"

But David, laughing, hit him away. Then he looked at Chuck.

"Maybe we won't be laughing when we land on Basidium. Chuck, do you remember how we felt when we first landed there and little Mebe and Oru came wailing over the horizon? It was just exactly *right*. I suppose it can't ever be that way again, but we helped Mebe and Oru and Ta and all his people, so maybe they'll help us. Except that now —" and David's voice trailed away. It was Wyrd he was thinking of, Wyrd, their enemy. Perhaps, no matter what Ta was willing to do, it could make no difference to Mr. Brumblydge. Maybe he was done for.

"Oh, there's no use thinking about it all the way there, Dave, or being scared or worried before we know how things are going to turn out," said Chuck sensibly, "so let's not bother ourselves."

"Chuck," said David after a few seconds of silence, "I've got something to tell you. You remember when
106

we got back from Mr. Bass's with the space ship, I ran in to get the bag of food and to tell Mom we were all set."

"Yep," said Chuck, and, thus reminded, he leaned over suddenly and dragged out the shopping bag of sandwiches and cake and fruit Mrs. Topman always insisted on packing for them. And presently they were sitting like kings, the galaxy spread before their eyes and in their hands thick wedges of Mrs. Topman's delicious angel food covered with thick chocolate icing and nuts all over.

His mouth full, David continued, "Well, I went in real quick to see how Mr. Brumblydge was doing, and he was still tossing and muttering and groaning something awful as if he just couldn't get any rest from what was going on in his head. So then, when I was going out, I looked down and saw a photograph sticking out from under the frill of that big chair near the door — you know, the one Mr. Brumblydge's jacket and pants were lying on before Mom hung them up. So maybe the photograph fell out of his jacket pocket. Anyway, I picked it up — and Chuck, I shouldn't have done it, but I didn't say anything to Mom or Dad because I was afraid they'd make me put it back and I wanted to show it to you. Well, I *will* put it back — but here it is —"

Chuck, having finished his cake, wiped his sticky

hands up and down on his cords. Then he turned on his flashlight and took the picture David was handing him, which turned out to be the old-fashioned kind of photograph known as a daguerreotype, a plain, brown photograph mounted on cardboard.

It was of two men. One was standing beside a pillar that had a large, potted fern on it. This man had his hand on the shoulder of the other who was sitting stiffly, solemnly upright in a heavily carved chair. There was a rose-patterned carpet beneath their slender, square-toed shoes, and on a screen behind them was a scene of Vesuvius erupting. The men wore rather full trousers and long frock coats that came to the knees and had nipped-in waists. Their cravats seemed to be of soft silk and were tied into large bows. The gentleman who was sitting down had on an exceedingly curly-brimmed top hat and seemed to be much older than the other man, for he had a full set of white side whiskers.

But what was so strange, so startling, was that the gentleman who was standing up, the dark, younger one, looked exactly like Prewytt Brumblydge in spite of his outlandish clothing.

"Dave — it *can't* be — !"

"I know. But turn over."

On the back was written in a spiky, crabbed hand, in faded purple ink, the words "Morgan Caerwen

108

and Prewytt M. Brumblydge, October 15, 1832."

"But that's — that's —" and Chuck was plainly trying to figure in his head, "*over a hundred and twenty years ago!*"

"Yes, and even then it looks as if he were maybe about thirty, and that would make him about a hundred and fifty years old now —"

"Well, but he can't be, Dave — he just *can't* be! Nobody one hundred and fifty years old could look the way Mr. Brumblydge does now, and nobody could even live that long. This must be his grandfather — or maybe his great-grandfather. I'll bet that'd be it."

David smiled an odd little smile.

"Chuck, take the flashlight and look at his forehead."

So Chuck peered close. And there on the forehead in the photograph was a tiny mark, and it was in pre-*cise*ly the spot where the Prewytt Brumblydge they knew had a birthmark on his forehead. And the living Prewytt Brumblydge had a cleft chin — and so did the Prewytt in the picture. The living Prewytt parted his hair on the left, and so did the other.

"Could a great-grandfather have *everything* just like his great-grandson?" wondered Chuck in unbelieving amazement.

"I don't know. Do you s'pose it would be Mr.

Brumblydge's great-*great*-grandfather who would have been a young man in 1832?"

Chuck stared at the photograph, studying every detail. Then: "Dave, what do you want to bet it's him — our P. Brumblydge, I mean?"

David was silent, but at last he said in a low voice, "Maybe we'll know everything when we get back home — about the photograph —"

"— and why he put the bones in the cliff instead of taking them back to Wales —" finished Chuck.

"That is, if we ever get home."

"What do you mean, Dave?"

"I mean, starting late. I keep thinking about it."

"Ho," said Chuck, "*that!* You sure do worry about everything. I told you it was only six seconds."

CHAPTER 14

A Slight Difference

ONLY six seconds, David thought to himself the instant he woke from that sudden sleep which always overtook the boys during the greater part of their journey to Basidium and again on the way home. Only six seconds. Had it mattered? Had they missed Basidium entirely?

No, they had not! Mr. Theo's excellent invention, the auto-reversatron, had turned their ship in midflight so that the tail rather than the nose now pointed downward for landing, and, just as David remembered from other journeys, they were no longer surrounded by the endless blackness of space, but by the pale, wavering, blue-green mists of the Mushroom Planet. They were safe. Never had the mists looked so beautiful. Already it seemed to him that he could catch the cool, fungusy smell that at home, whenever he put his nose to a box of mushrooms, sent a sharp stab of longing and excitement through him.

112

His pulse beat hard with happy expectation. He leaned forward to gaze down through the big window — and there it was — their little planet.

"Chuck! Chuck! Wake up — we're here! We're all right!"

Yes, and this always came next: the jolt of wondrous surprise at his own voice, a tinkle of wind chimes, high and queer and only faintly like his usual voice. Then came amazement that he should really be speaking a language that neither he nor Chuck could ever remember once they were home again on earth, that they had never learned, and that seemed to be given them as a gift while they slept.

At the same time Chuck, laughing at David's voice, leaned forward beside him. Then David pressed the button that sent that furious explosion of flame belching out beneath them so that their swift descent would be slowed and their ship could land safely. Down it came with a gentle thud, cushioned on the green and spongy surface.

But by this time Chuck was no longer laughing.

David had his head down, busy with the controls of the ship. Then he was stooping over, trying to get the big shopping bag of food out from under his seat so that they could take something to eat with them. The roar of the ship's landing had ceased. Everything was still as it usually is on Basidium, for there all sounds are muffled by the eternally hovering fogs. But at Chuck's silence David glanced up.

"We've made a mistake," announced Chuck flatly. "The six seconds *did* make a difference." David's heart seemed to stop entirely. "We're in a city, but it's not Ta's city — it's another."

David straightened and stared down at what lay beyond the grove of mushrooms in which they had landed. There, spread out before them, were buildings that seemed to be fashioned entirely of a reddish-brown stone rather than the pale, porous rock the Basidiumites used. And this city seemed to be a vast place with what looked like winding streets, and David could see that a few of the buildings were curiously high and peaked, others oblong or square with irregular tops. But none of them were domed as the Basidiumites' homes were, so that it was as if the people of these two cities had nothing to do with each other at all.

"Dave, what if the people here don't like us? What if they —" But he did not finish the sentence. "Does it seem queer down there to you?"

"You mean, it looks as if there aren't any roofs?"

"Yes, the buildings look hollow and dark, though it's sort of hard to tell because of the mushrooms growing around and because it's shadowy. I wonder why nobody comes out."

114

"Maybe the noise of the ship scared them so much they don't dare. Maybe they're hiding."

"Shall we open the door and see if we can hear anything? Shall we get out, Dave?"

"I don't know. They might take us prisoners. Still, they could just as well be friendly the way the Mushroom People are. Chuck, you know what? I've always wanted to really explore Basidium. I've always wondered if maybe there were other towns on it beside Ta's. Mr. Bass said that though Basidium's only thirty-five miles in diameter, its area is 3,846 square miles, so it seemed to me there'd have to be more than one city."

For some little time Chuck studied the silent buildings that lay beyond the mushroom grove.

"Dave, you know what I think? We don't have to be afraid. Because I'll bet you anything there's nobody down there. I think those are all ruins — I think it's a dead city."

"You mean like the ones Miss Pilchard told us about — like Angkor Thom and Angkor Vat in Cambodia?"

Chuck nodded, and a sudden chill rippled down David's arms, but at once he felt a sharp surge of impatience.

"Come on, then — let's explore. Oh, but first — what about our folks? We promised Dad we'd signal

115

the minute we got here. Do you think we should tell that we've come down in a strange city, and that maybe we're — that maybe —"

"We're lost?" said Chuck in his downright fashion. "No, I don't. It'd just worry them and how do we know, Dave — it *could* be that Ta's city isn't very far away. Let's just signal that we've landed safely. That's the truth, anyway, and it'll satisfy them for now."

So they signaled and then quickly, breathlessly, they unbolted the door and in flowed the damp, fungus-smelling air of Basidium. Chuck stood poised in the doorway, then let himself down over the side landing unhurt eight feet below, and a second later David dropped down beside him.

They stood in a grove of tall thick-stemmed gray and pink and cream mushrooms as well as smaller, more delicate kinds with velvety brown tops and rich vermilion undersides. On some of the hoods of the mushrooms there were streaks of pale green striping the brown, and some of the creamy ones were dusted with a pale golden sheen and the flutings beneath their hoods were a deep copper. Beyond this grove was another of primitive, fern-like trees, leafless, but with spongy, serrated fronds and smooth, thin stems. And beneath these was a dappled shade from the pale, pale shine of earth, only

116

now beginning to receive the first faint rays of the sun on its eastern side.

They listened. Silence — silence — silence — almost a waiting silence, David thought. Now they were at the edge of the fern grove, but no cries of alarm went up, no missiles came whistling through the air, no creature showed himself. Only the lalas, small flying lizards, as well as other little flying things the boys had never seen before, flashed bronze and garnet-red and cobalt-blue above their heads, making churring noises like the snapping of rubber bands.

Quietly, David and Chuck stepped out into the open, and as they went closer, they saw that this was indeed a place of the departed, a city of ruin. Blocks of stone had fallen where once were ways for walking, pillars stood alone that had been joined by arches, fungi of all kinds had sprung from cracks and crevices.

Then at last they came within full view of the first of the buildings, and what they saw upon the side of the wall that faced them caused them to stop in stunned awe, to stand there speechless trying to understand how such a thing as this could possibly be.

The City of Silence

For upon that wall, which was made of numberless blocks of stone fitted carefully together, was a carving. And this carving was so finely and deeply cut, the colors that filled in the picture were so rich and vivid, that there could be no mistaking what it was.

It was a sun, a big flaring sun with rays. And though, in places, large patches of green mold had spread across the wall, it could still be seen that, ranged around the sun in different orbits, were eight planets.

The sun and its rays were gold, as if gold dust had been worked into the very surface of the stone. The smallest sphere, plainly Mercury, in an orbit nearest the sun, was a deep red. Then came a yellow Venus as if to show that this is the brightest of the planets. Next was a lapis-lazuli-blue earth with a white moon and a tiny blue-green Basidium; then came an orange Mars; next, a pale, huge, silvery Jupiter with a red jewel of Basidium set into it to indicate the

118

Great Red Spot; then a pale yellow Saturn with green and blue and red rings; and last of all a great green Uranus and a greater green Neptune.

There it was, a magnificent, richly colored, quite accurate picture of the solar system — except for the absence of little Pluto. Then David saw it: still another, outer orbit traced in gold, and, only a bit of it showing beneath a fan of fungus — what must have been the remotest planet. David broke the fungus away and rubbed the stone clear with his hand, and yes, there was Pluto. It could have been nothing else.

"But I don't understand. How could they have known?" gasped Chuck. "Why, astronomers on earth only discovered Pluto in —"

"I think about 1930," said David. "So then these people must have had telescopes —"

"But these ruins look so ancient! Why, maybe they've been here for thousands of years. It looks as if they have."

"Like the Mayan and Incan ruins."

"Dave, maybe we're the first people ever to set foot here since this civilization passed away."

Again David felt the cold shiver ripple over him.

"But they couldn't have had telescopes, Chuck — not if they're that old."

"Why not?" demanded Chuck. "Why not — anything? And they *must* have had telescopes. That's the solar system they've painted, isn't it?"

Yes, it was. And what else, what other wonders lay within those silent walls? David put an eager hand on Chuck's arm and pulled him away. Perhaps they were lost. They had no idea what lay between them and Ta's city; the purpose of this journey to Basidium, to get Brumblium for Prewytt, was almost forgotten. What consumed them now was curiosity about the people here on this planet who had known of the solar system in centuries and centuries gone by.

Now, with widened eyes and baited breaths, David and Chuck entered the great ruined building itself.

"Dave, this must have been the temple where they studied the stars."

There were no objects here, no remains of furniture or ornaments of any kind. The spacious, paved stretch of floor was empty, but around the edges were terraces, or steps, of various heights and widths, some narrow and some broad, so that perhaps, the boys thought, these were used for sitting and for writing and study. If these people had used tablets to write on, they would not have needed tables.

On the walls, splotched over with moss and mold, were more tremendous, richly colored pictures of the heavens. There were gold stars in a deep blue background, a swarm of what must have been the asteroids between Mars and Jupiter, a fiery comet with a long, blazing tail, and a great Saturn close up showing its vast rings. And the rings — wonder of wonders — were not solid, but were composed of infinite numbers of tiny particles, tiny satellites, as the astronomers on earth have finally discovered them to be.

"But these people *must* have had telescopes, Chuck, and all kinds of other instruments besides, to discover Pluto and to know that the rings of Saturn are made up of millions and millions of little satellites. Mr. Bass said our astronomers were only sure of that after they'd analyzed the light of the rings with a spectroscope."

But an even deeper mystery awaited them. The floor seemed to be all of a royal blue, but, hidden under growths like pale, spreading hands of brown, pink and cream, they now made out what seemed to be dozens of globes of gold, spirals and whirlpools of gold which could not have been anything but galaxies. For they were precisely like those photographs of galaxies which Mr. Bass had taken with his star camera. What was more, there were red lines of different lengths darting outward among the galaxies and it looked as if the artist had meant to show that

121

all of them were hurrying away — outward — from one another.

"Dave, do you remember Mr. Bass telling us that some astronomers think that everything in the universe is rushing away from everything else in it at the rate of millions of miles an hour? He called it the 'expanding universe.' "

"Yes, and he said that the far-off galaxies must be traveling away even faster, maybe at the speed of light itself, and the tremendously distant ones at *more* than the speed of light, because the farther away they are, the faster they go. Can it be possible that these people knew that, Chuck? They *must* have!"

Chuck simply shook his head and, in increasing wonderment, the boys now went out and wandered from building to building. All — all were empty save for the terraces around the sides of the rooms and always on the walls were the vivid paintings. But never any paintings of people: only of the heavens, or scenes of this lost valley of Basidium with high mountains around it and the mists winding, of the plants and animals — the hairy morunbend and others Chuck and David had never seen, and the little flying creatures. Not all of the colors were strong; some were delicate and soft, but as clear as though, indeed, they had been painted only yesterday.

Now they came to the first of the tall, curiously pointed buildings, or towers, which the boys had seen from the space ship. Its walls sloped until they met, twenty feet up, in a blunted peak, and when David and Chuck ventured into the inner gloom they saw that the walls were very thick and that these must have been storage towers. For here, piled high, were enormous chests and at the foot of the pile smaller chests of all sizes. They seemed to be made of some kind of metal.

"Chuck, now maybe we can find things that belonged to these people — money and jewelry and maybe even statuettes so that we can see what they looked like!"

In furious hope they attacked one chest after another, vainly wrenching at the lids of those they could reach. But the metal, whatever it was, was not like the gold that had been ground to a dust and worked into the stone walls where the great pictures had been painted. For it was so covered with verdigris (a greenish-gray deposit on bronze or brass) that the chests were dark with it and the lids stuck tight. Now and again they might force one of the lids to move a fraction of an inch; they might wrench one up, but only a little and not nearly enough to catch even a glimpse of what was inside. At last, with scratched fingers and broken nails, they had to admit that it was no use.

Then suddenly Chuck picked up one of the smallest chests as though to dash it to the ground, and as he did so it clinked as if it were filled with all sorts of small things.

"Bash it, Chuck! Bash it against the wall!"

Which Chuck did, as mightily as he could, and part of his strength was made up of frustrated, impatient anger. Whereupon the lid broke open and from the chest spilled what seemed to be dozens of disks that chinked as they fell together.

What a mad scrabbling there was then! Outside in the light David and Chuck found that they held in their hands circular seals or amulets, flat on the bottom and with domed tops, carved of the same stones as had been strung together in Ta's necklace and in all the different colors of those stones, the rich and strange colors of the jewels of Basidium. Each amulet was exactly the same size, about an inch and a half across and all were in the shape of mushroom heads or half-balls. Each had deep lines cut into it on the domed top which crossed at the center so that the dome was divided into pie-shaped wedges, and in each one of these wedges was a different, curious carved design or picture. On every amulet one of these pictures was always a mushroom.

"Mushroom Stones!" whispered Chuck.

"But how *can* they be — I mean, how —?"

To behold duplicates of a single, odd little object from one small corner of earth here on this satellite of earth, thousands of miles away from it in space, and in a storage chest which must have been frozen shut for centuries in this lost and ruined city, was something at least as impossible, seemingly, as those paintings on the walls and floor of the Sky Temple.

"I think we're dreaming, Dave," said Chuck at last. "I just don't think any of this is really happening."

But when David gave him a sharp punch on the arm, Chuck had to admit that perhaps it was.

Eagerly the boys plunged their hands into the chest again and again and, as they emptied it, came across what must have been a compass. They found one or two rulers (or at least they were flat and straight and narrow with markings at intervals), some knives, a small mallet, some little plates, a necklace, three rings exquisitely carved, two bracelets of links most intricately woven together, pots with hinged lids, beautifully shaped, and a long thin metal stick with a claw at the end that might have been a back-scratcher.

But no statuettes. Never any likenesses of people, as though in that faraway, lost time it had been thought a sin to make any image of a thinking being. Or perhaps this race, that had been capable of making telescopes with which to study the planets and stars, had been afraid to make images of themselves because of some superstition.

"Let's carry back all we can in our pockets, Chuck." But as he began stowing away as much of the treasure hoard as he could, David found himself asking, "Back where?" For even if they took off for earth precisely two hours after landing as they always had, they would not be starting from their usual spot near Ta's city. And so wouldn't this make a difference when it came to returning? Certainly it didn't seem likely they would land on Cap'n Tom's beach. But what was the good of worrying about that now? As Chuck would say, he always seemed to be worrying about *something*.

They were by now near the center of the city. And no sooner had they started out once again to explore further into the ruins than they heard a grunting and snuffling that David knew immediately he had heard somewhere before.

"The morunbend, Chuck — the big thing. We saw it the first time we were on Basidium, and the second too. Listen!"

126

For a moment the stillness was intense, then again came the coughing and grunting, not of one morunbend, but of many, and now there were dull thuds and shufflings. Chuck stared at David in horror.

"It's — they're coming closer — maybe a whole herd —"

At once the boys started running. And then in an empty, ruined square they stopped to glance back, and through fallen walls they saw them: the same slothlike creatures they had glimpsed on their other two journeys, but then only fleetingly and at a distance. Now the heads of the morunbends turned, and David knew instantly that they had been seen, for the whole herd, about twenty animals, began moving rapidly toward them along the empty streets, uttering loud, hoarse cries rather like barks. Whereupon the boys turned once more and ran in terror as fast as they could toward a mountain slope that rose not far off near the outskirts of the city. But each time they changed their course through the ruined streets, the morunbends did also.

The boys darted up the slope, and the higher they went the more scattered the groves of giant mushrooms became, until, when they reached an open place they paused to look back once again. And there on the edge of the city they saw the huddle of dark, hunched shapes with short necks and long heads still moving toward them, two or three ahead of the others. They came at a steady pace without stopping for anything, their woolly backs bobbing up and down as though they had been a herd of bison. They came on relentlessly as if each animal shared a single thought.

"Hurry, Chuck, hurry! Look, there's a big, dark crack in the rocks up there — maybe we could hide —"

Gasping for breath, the perspiration running down their white faces, they came finally to a tall, very narrow opening in the steep and rocky face of the mountain. In they went.

"Keep going back, Dave — back as far as you can until it gets so narrow they can't follow. I can hear them — they're still coming —"

The boys pressed on into the mountain through the cleft, a subterranean crack between two giant rocks so narrow now that no morunbend could possibly have gotten himself in, until at last they were wedging themselves sideways. But then to the boys' astonishment the crack widened and by the very dim light that remained they could see that it became a tunnel, a winding passageway, and at once Chuck snapped on his flashlight.

"Why, it looks just like that passageway we followed through the mountain with Mr. Bass and Mr.

128

Theo and Ta and Mebe and Oru the last time we were here, when the big main entrance to the Hall of the Ancient Ones caved in and we had to get out another way!"

"Then maybe we're going to be all right, after all. Look, there's black stuff on the ceiling as if people with burning flares had come this way." David reached up and ran his finger through it, and it came off as if it were soot.

"Let's go on in. That soot could have been there for hundreds of years," said Chuck, plainly trying to be as sensible as possible to keep them both from being too hopeful. "At least we can't go back, with those morunbends out there, so the only thing is to go on into the mountain."

Which they did.

At first they talked excitedly about the lost city and the marvelous things they had seen, trying to find some explanation for those amazing paintings and for the amulets, the Mushroom Stones so precisely like the one Mr. Bass had shown them on earth. But as time went on, a heavy silence grew between them. There seemed no end to this cold, dark passageway, everlastingly winding, leading up sudden slopes, dropping, narrowing to slits scarcely wide enough to squeeze through, then opening out again, the roof lowering until they had to crawl on

129

their hands and knees, then giving way once more.

It seemed to David that now mile upon mile of solid mountain, tons of it, must be pressing upon the rock just above their heads, for he felt trapped and suffocated. He longed to shout at the top of his lungs, in pure fear, that they should turn and run back as fast as possible. And yet, perhaps they were almost at the end of their journey, he kept reminding himself. And he tried to think of encouraging things, fortunate possibilities, but why was it so hard to think of these and so easy to let himself be overcome with despair?

"Shall we go back, Dave?" asked Chuck suddenly in such a voice that David knew that he too had been sick at his stomach because of these same thoughts.

"I guess not," David managed to get out, but the instant he spoke, Chuck stopped and put a hand on his arm.

"Listen!"

David felt his ears prick forward like an animal's, and it seemed to him he heard — very, very faintly — a murmur, the far-off rise and fall of what could have been a voice.

The next moment David was plunged into darkness, for Chuck, in his desperate excitement, had darted on ahead, taking the light with him, so that David was left to feel along the side of the pitch-black tunnel as best he could. Shouting after Chuck in his fury, he kept on, however, bumping into turnings, stumbling on sudden upward slopes or downturns, and running against rocks he had to climb. But now, through his own angry protests, he heard:

"Guess what, Dave — guess what!"

Up ahead, through an opening in the rock, David was certain he spied a faint gleam, a kind of soft shining, as though on the other side of that rock it was day. Yet, no — for the light wavered, faded, and then brightened again. What could it be? Now Chuck turned his flashlight so that David could see the way, and when they came together, far, far more wonderful than the light, David was sure he heard a voice asking a startled question. He held his breath. Yes, for there came an answering voice, a silence, then a bewildered question again.

"Chuck, who is it? It — *can't* be —"

But those voices were blessedly familiar.

CHAPTER 16

A Nice Little Problem in Arithmetic

WHEN David put his head through the opening beside Chuck's and stared down, what he beheld was a scene he had longed for with all his heart but had not even dared to let himself imagine.

There, far beneath them, on the floor of the enormous cavern, whose high ceiling was lost to view in shadows above them and whose walls were thickly encrusted with rough chunks of the jewels of Basidium, stood Ta, the king. His great bald head was tilted back and he was gazing upward in alarm. Not far below, on the wall of the cavern, was little Mr. Theo, Tyco Bass's younger cousin, climbing as rapidly as he could toward the opening from where the boys' voices must have been heard as they shouted back and forth to one another. And in spite of the high excitement of the moment, David was struck at once by the fact that he was no longer dressed in the shabby but elegant slim-legged trousers, vest and opera cloak he'd had on when he first came from

132

earth, but had taken over those palely colored robes such as Ta was wearing.

The moment after their faces came into view, Ta uttered such a cry of stunned amazement that Mr. Theo almost lost his grip. Then, he, too, tilted back his head, large and bald like Ta's, in order to discover the reason for this sudden exclamation. When he saw Chuck and David he had to hang on tight while he made sure he was not dreaming or hadn't taken leave of his senses.

"*David!*" burst from him. "*Chuck!* Why, how in the name of goodness —"

"Oh, Mr. Theo, we're so *glad* to see you!" cried David. How good it was to look once more into that small face, so like Tyco's, with its usually alert, humorous expression now replaced by the most intense astonishment.

"We thought we were done for," shouted Chuck. "We thought we'd never get out of that darned tunnel, Mr. Theo, and I kept thinking what if we were lost inside the mountain —"

Mr. Theo clung to his precarious perch, his great eyes wider than ever. But after a moment he seemed to gather his wits again.

"Now you must listen to me," he said. "I will go down and you come after me slowly and very carefully along this crevice. It is the only way you can

133

make it. But wait until I get right down so that I can watch and advise you where to put your feet, because if you make one false step there is nothing I can do to help you." Whereupon he began backing, while Ta looked on in taut silence, plainly having no wish by any further outcries to add to the touchiness of the situation. When Mr. Theo had landed safely, there were more shoutings back and forth and then the boys gingerly climbed down, working their way according to Mr. Theo's instructions. A few minutes later all four of them were together.

Almost overcome by their unexpected arrival at the Hall of the Ancient Ones and, more than this, by their seemingly miraculous reunion with Ta and Mr. Theo, the boys could only fling their arms around their two friends. They forgot entirely Ta's royal dignity, that air of majesty about him, which was so enhanced by the necklace of great, richly hued stones that hung about his neck.

They kept shouting, "We're here! We're really here! Everything's all right after all!" And then, "But, Mr. Theo, where are your cape and top hat and white gloves?" for these articles of clothing had meant Mr. Theo to them.

"Oh, I had to give them up," he said. "They were quite unsuitable for Basidium. And indeed I find these soft, plastic-like robes much more comfortable and easier to get around in." But he still, David noticed happily, combed forward the fringe of hair around his bald pate in that funny, old-fashioned way he had always done. And he still managed, somehow, a look of style.

Mr. Theo's joy was plainly as great as theirs and, as for Ta, he, like Mr. Theo, returned their embraces warmly.

"My young friends, what you must have been through! How did you find the entrance to the mountain on the other side? Where did you land that you were able to come across this ancient and long-unused approach to our Hall? How thankful I am that you're safe!"

So then David and Chuck, unable to keep from interrupting each other, but managing anyway to get out the whole unbelievable story, told Ta and Mr. Theo all about landing in that silent valley on the other side of the mountain. They described the buildings as they had looked from the window of the space ship, how Chuck had had a feeling that this was a dead city, a lost city. And when they told Ta and Mr. Theo about that marvelous carved painting on the side of the first wall they had come to, the two little men stared at one another as though they could scarcely credit their ears, and Ta cried,

"At last — at last — at last!"

135

"And it's *all* ruined, Great Ta — nobody's there — not a soul," David plunged on, "and we saw paintings of the solar system, and galaxies — but how could this be? Who painted them? And we found —"

"— treasure!" shouted Chuck, almost beside himself with the splendid excitement of being able to tell Ta and Mr. Theo such an unbelievable story about their own planet. "Treasure in the tall, pointed storage towers, only we couldn't get the chests open, except one little one absolutely *full* of Mushroom

Stones. Here, look at this —" and he and David drew handfuls of the disks from their pockets and held them under the open mouths and wondering eyes of the other two. "Mr. Theo, *how* could Mr. Bass have a Mushroom Stone exactly like —"

But at this moment, David took hold of Chuck's arm.

"Chuck," he said, "we've got to get the Brumblium. We can't stay. What about Mr. Brumblydge? He's so sick that if we don't get home as soon as

possible, he may not even — he may not — well, anyhow, we *can't* wait another twenty-four hours, and we'll have to if we don't leave Basidium in just about an hour."

"Mr. Brumblydge is sick, you say!" exclaimed Ta.

"Yes, Great Ta, he's awfully sick," returned David. "That's why we signaled Mebe and Oru to ask if we could come, and they said they had no right to say anything because you and Mr. Theo weren't there, so we just took a chance and came anyway. My dad, who takes care of sick people, can't seem to do a thing for Mr. Brumblydge —"

"— and so we thought maybe if we got the Brumblium for him so that he could go ahead with his experiments and his Theory of the Universe, that would help," finished Chuck.

"Theo," said Ta, "we must get back to the city at once. We have been here," he went on to explain to the boys, at the same time taking down a flare from its holder on the wall of the cavern, "asking the blessing of the Ancient Ones and their consent to an extremely grave decision of mine. It came to me in answer to this whole problem of your taking our metal, which we call Grillia and which you call Brumblium, for the magician on the Great Protector — your Mr. Prewytt Brumblydge. Now this decision of mine is so momentous that I wanted Theo here

138

with me as witness to the answer from my ancestors. This we have just received, the one answer I had hoped for. All I need is the blessing of my people — and yours, my friends," he added unexpectedly.

"*Ours*, Great Ta!" David and Chuck repeated in astonishment.

But Ta was bent upon getting on with things and had already leaped ahead in his thinking.

"The Creature of Silver," he continued quickly, and he meant the space ship, "where is it?"

"Oh!" and David clapped his hand over his mouth. "It's way back there, clear on the other side of the mountain in the Lost City —"

"Very well," said Ta. "Can Theo find it?"

"Yes, he can," replied Chuck. "Here's my flashlight, Mr. Theo, to go through the mountain with. Then when you get out, you just cut right across through the ruins to where the space ship is sticking up. You can't miss it. But what'll you do after that?"

"Ah," said Mr. Theo, taking the flashlight, "that remains to be seen. But I believe," he said, and there was that alert, pointed look David remembered from their very first meeting, that feeling about him of quiet ability, "I believe that what I have before me is an extremely nice little problem in arithmetic. The space ship must be made to go up at pre-*cise*ly the right angle and to pre-*cise*ly the right height, so that

I can come down again on pre-*cise*ly the spot at which you were supposed to have landed in the first place. I won't ask you how you chanced to miss, because it might take too long. Instead I shall start out at once and do my figuring as I go through the mountain. I shall see you all later in good time for the take-off."

He gave them a cheery gesture of farewell, tucked the flashlight away in his robes, and began rapidly scaling the wall of the cavern.

When he reached the top, Ta called up, "No stopping to explore by the wayside once you get to the Lost City, now, Theo!" But he spoke in such a warm, affectionate voice that the boys knew he was only teasing his friend.

"I shall be stern with myself, Great Ta, and look forward to the time when we can explore it together," promised Mr. Theo, smiling down at them. Then he vanished into the opening.

The Grave Decision

Now Ta and the boys set out in the greatest possible haste for Ta's city. As they went, first along the winding corridors of the Hall of the Ancient Ones where Ta's flare drew dazzling flashes of all hues from the jewel-encrusted walls, the boys spilled out their story. And so lost were they in describing the wonders they had seen, and so entranced was Ta by their telling (interrupting their story from time to time to put questions which seemed to have been in his mind for many, many years) that the boys were hardly aware of the length of their journey. Ta walked between them, setting the pace with his long, rapid stride which caused the handsome necklace about his neck to swing backwards and forwards upon his chest. This necklace was a twin of the one he had given them out of gratitude on their first journey to Basidium.

"The Lost City," said Ta at length, "has been known among my people since before the time of our fathers. But none have seen it — it has been a forbidden place because of tales of harm that would come to him who tried to seek it out.

"Since I was young I have longed to find it, but always my Wise Men, those before Mebe and Oru, advised against my going. But when your good Theo came to live among us and heard these tales, nothing would do but that both of us, he and I together, should set out to discover it. Many and many a sacra Theo and I have traveled in search of the Lost City. And on our last trip, we came to the top of a high ridge, and there, at the bottom of a sheer drop of almost a sacra and a half, we looked down on that place we had been seeking so long.

"Simply to behold those ruins, the long walls and tall, peaked towers which you say are storage places, told me that this was the city of a people far greater than my own.

"In order to build those towers and walls, which still stand, they had conquered, in some mysterious fashion of their own, the terrible strength of the mushrooms which continually break up and push aside after a time whatever we erect. This method I must discover — Theo and I shall find it out, now that you have told us of possibly the one and only way into the Lost City.

"And those richly colored paintings of the heavenly bodies that have still not perished after so unthinkably long a time: from these too I know that the lost people were far, far ahead of us. It makes me sad, because I understand now that we are what remain of a once noble race."

"But what could have happened to them, Great Ta?" asked Chuck. "Dave and I tried to figure it out when we were coming through the mountain — I guess to keep ourselves from thinking we were lost and might never get out of there. Anyway, we wondered if maybe they knew an enemy was coming and packed all they owned away in those storage towers. Then maybe they were defeated and all of them were killed —"

"But if they *were* defeated," David broke in, "why didn't the enemy ransack the storage towers, and take over the city or destroy it? And who *was* the enemy?"

"Who was the enemy, David?" returned Ta in a strange tone. "I think it was not the kind that could unlock chests and destroy buildings. Do you remember what happened to my people when the sulfur plants at the Place of Hidden Water were shriveled by the Great Heat at the time of your first journey here?"

The boys nodded, and David saw again the huge, anxious eyes and pale faces of the little Basidiumites.

143

Only the Basidiumite children, given what few sulfur plants were left from the last Time of New Growth, had kept their healthy green. For the secret was that without those plants, without that small amount of sulfur in their diets which each fresh crop provided, the Mushroom People sickened and died.

"So it was some Great Heat of long ago that was the enemy, is that it?"

"I don't know for certain, Chuck. But so the story has come down through my family. They could have fought a living enemy. But a change of climate that took their sulfur from them — this they were helpless against. One by one, after storing their treasures, they fell. And at last the few remaining lay listening to the silence of their deserted city, knowing that that silence might last forever." Ta drew a deep sigh. "The grandeur of those beings is no more."

"But, Great Ta," exclaimed David, thinking to himself that that grandeur still lived in this most remarkable person, "when we told you about the sun and the planets and the galaxies we'd seen in the paintings, you knew what we were talking about."

"Why, of course," replied Ta, his eyes lighting, "but only because Theo has been teaching me all he knows ever since he came. In his Place of Mysteries, which you call an observatory, he and I have spent many Times of Light and Dark speaking of the won-

144

ders of the endless bowl that curves over us, and of life on the Great Protector which is your home. You know, there is one thing he told me about which I can scarcely believe. I wonder if you have heard of it — the Hole in Space —"

David and Chuck nodded. Oh, they had, indeed!

"Is it possible?" exclaimed Ta in wonderment. "Theo described it to me as an awesome thing that travels in an orbit around your own world. And he said that it goes at an enormous speed — far, far faster than this planet travels or that other pale one which you call the moon."

"Yes, and *that's* why," said Chuck, "we have to leave home at pre-*cise*ly midnight, and why we can stay here only two hours — no more — no less —"

"Otherwise," Ta took him up, "you would, if you started late, be caught in the path of that whirling, magnetic force, and be dragged, sucked, plunged into — what? The negative universe, Theo says. *The Back of the Beyond!*" and Ta's eyes shone "My friends, this is to be the subject of Theo's and my next talk. Oh, there's no end to what he has told me, and what he will yet tell me. He himself says that he has only just begun. How *good* my life is now that he is here — I can never express my thanks to you for bringing him! In fact, it was he who first kindled that spark which lighted my strong desire to — but

145

you shall hear of this soon enough, for I see that we have almost arrived."

As they approached the city, Ta's people streamed forth to meet him with much rejoicing. And they were all bald-headed and dressed in robes like Ta's, though theirs were shorter than his. Many of them were playing those golden flutes which the Basidiumites call maleetles, and a company of others were singing those strange, haunting harmonies, in a minor key, which the boys remembered from their other journeys. All of them seemed happy and lighthearted — that is, until they came close enough to realize it was Chuck and David who were with their king.

Then they stopped; their voices as well as the flute-song died away. They turned to each other in fright, and David could hear them asking if these beings from the Great Protector had flown like the lalas from their far world without need of the Creature of Silver.

But now there came a sudden roaring out of the sky, whereupon everyone craned his neck and stared upward to where a streak of light could be seen descending out of the mists, a streak that seemed to be sitting upon an orange-red jet of flame. A second

146

later the streak disappeared beyond the horizon, the roar ceased — and then what a terror-stricken hubbub arose!

"The Creature of Silver! The Creature of Silver! It is the magician, come to get the Grillia! He will take us into his power — what shall we do, Great Ta — what shall we do?"

"*SILENCE!*" roared Ta.

And there *was* silence. They all lifted grave, wondering faces.

"Listen to me, foolish ones. Our guests, here by my side, came in the Creature of Silver, as always. How else could they arrive? But they landed elsewhere than in the usual place. As Theo is not with me, it should be plain to you that he is the one who has brought it to the city. Let me hear no more from your silly mouths."

So once again the playing and singing continued, and the procession entered the palace, round-roofed like an igloo and exactly like the other buildings of the city except that it was much larger. Here, just as David remembered from his and Chuck's first journey to Basidium, all was quiet and peaceful. Dried plants — sweet-smelling fronds — were strewn over the floor of the long, spacious main hall, which was lighted by flares set into the walls of pinkish-gray

148

blocks of light, porous stone. The whole room was flooded by a soft radiance.

At once Ta went to his golden chair at the head of the hallway and motioned Chuck and David to sit on low steps at his left hand. And now little Mebe and Oru appeared and, in a rush of high-pitched exclamations, expressed their joy at seeing David and Chuck once again. David thought with affection that they sounded like two excited squirrels.

Then food was brought them, but at the same moment Mr. Theo arrived, quite out of breath from having hurried to the palace from where he had landed the space ship. The instant he saw the boys through the press of people, he raised both hands and lifted his eyebrows in an expression of wonderment at all he had beheld in the Lost City. Then he came forward and took his place at their sides just below Ta's throne. All around on the floor, cross-legged on the mats of dried fronds, the Basidiumites arranged themselves with much murmuring and gesturing throughout the length of the hall.

"You must have figured just pre-*cise*ly right, Mr. Theo," David leaned over to whisper in tremendous admiration, while Ta was busy giving various orders to members of the palace staff.

"Well, of course I did — I knew I had to," he

whispered back with a touch of pride. "The only difficulty was keeping my mind on my business as I went through the ruined streets, and I'll have to admit that temptation sorely beset me. *Imagine* being surrounded by mysteries and wonders that I have dreamed of ever since Ta first told me of the City, and then to be unable to explore them! It was cruel, I can tell you! By the way, did you boys happen to run into a pack of morunbends?"

David and Chuck started, for they had completely forgotten to warn Mr. Theo.

"Oh, did you — did they —?" began David.

But at the guilty look on the boys' faces, Mr. Theo burst out laughing. "They chased you, I imagine. But do you know why? The morunbend is the timidest, friendliest, most curious animal you can think of — timid when he's by himself, but when he's with others of his kind, so friendly and curious that he will not let you alone. A morunbend in a herd will even leave his food in order to be patted and made over — but, speaking of eating, you must begin at once and try everything. You see those slices of pale pink mushroom? You will find they taste deliciously like ripe avocado, and the deeper pink just a little like roast chicken. The pale green will seem to you like the most heavenly cheesecake you've ever had in your lives, and the brown almost like pineapple sher-
150

bet. There, now — I think that Ta is about to begin."

"My people," began Ta in a quiet, far-reaching voice, "there is no need for me to relate to you the events that led up to my going with our good friend, Theo, to the Hall of the Ancient Ones. All that I need tell you is that I went there to ask permission of them to carry out a decision concerning the metal of which our world is mostly made, and the giving of a small part of it to the magician on the Great Protector.

"Now I find that he is gravely ill and needs the encouragement which our gift of Grillia could bring him — perhaps in order to save his life. But this magician, this Brumblydge, seems to be one who burns like fire with new and strange thoughts, who is restless as the wind, whose mind will not cease from delving into hidden matters. What will he do with our metal, and will good come from his work with it, or disaster? Can he be trusted to come here some day and take our metal for the use of those on the Great Protector?

"These questions are the reasons for my decision, which is this. My people: I, myself, must go to that far world and take pieces of Grillia with me. And know this also, that the Ancient Ones have given me their blessings and have said that it shall be so."

At these unexpected words, there was a sharp indrawing of breath from all over the long hall; everyone's eyes grew huge and mouths fell open and stayed that way. But before any protests could be raised, Ta continued:

"I must go back with our guests in the Creature of Silver so that I can look into the face of the magician with my own eyes and know that, if he ever comes here, he will do us no harm — for it may be that he will build his own Creature of Silver. I must speak with him myself. I must make sure that he is such a one as Theo has proved to be, such a one as our friends are who once saved our lives and for whom we must do good in return if we possibly can. There is no other way but for me to make the journey, and I will have to admit to you that I am eager for it and look forward to it with the greatest happiness.

"Do I hear your welcomes, David and Chuck?"

So astonished had the boys been throughout the last part of Ta's speech that for a moment they could not utter a single word. And as Ta's people were absolutely stunned by the breath-taking proposal of their king, there was, for perhaps one second, a dead silence.

Then everyone began exclaiming at once.

"We welcome you, Great Ta!" shouted Chuck, jumping up and going to his side in enormous excitement. "We welcome you to the Great Protector! Oh, boy, just *wait* 'till you see all we've got to show you! Just think, Mr. Theo, of all the things —"

"How long will you stay?" demanded David, just barely able to keep himself from grabbing Ta by the arm in his eagerness to know. "And will Mr. Theo come? Gee whillikers, what'll Prewytt Brumblydge say when we bring you! I can just imagine his face —"

And meanwhile, from the Basidiumites, who were now on their feet and milling about singly and in groups, words and phrases shot up as from a surging sea.

"No, no! He must not go — he is our king —"

"The Great Ta will be killed — he will be lost and never come back again — what would become of us?"

"Yes, but the Ancient Ones have said he shall go, and if they have said a thing, it must be done —"

"But what if a trick should be played and the magician should change him into an animal, and he himself come back in the shape of the Great Ta to rule over us?"

"But the Ancient Ones would know this. They see into the future, and there can be no harm if the Ancient Ones have given their blessing. Our king is strong and courageous and wise, and when he comes back he will be able to tell us of having flown through nothingness. What an honor it will be to us to have a king who has flown, who has walked upon a world beyond this one, and who has seen the boxes Theo has told us of — the ones with living faces and voices hidden in them —!"

"Yes, Great Ta, you shall go. The Ancient Ones have said it, and Theo shall be our leader while you are away. We give you our blessing, too."

"How much time is left?" asked Ta instantly, turning to the boys.

"Fifteen minutes," replied Chuck, who had just glanced at his watch with a sudden stab of anxiety. And Ta must have learned about earth time as well as about the Hole in Space and a multitude of other matters, from Mr. Theo, for he nodded.

"Good!" he said. "Then we cannot wait for those long-drawn-out farewells that I find so painful. We must leave at once."

In that moment David saw that his face was alight like a boy's who is about to start at last on the greatest and highest adventure of his whole life.

PART THREE

A Stranger to Earth

CHAPTER 18

The Arrival of Ta

Dᴀᴠɪᴅ thought his mother was going to faint when she first set eyes on the King of the Mushroom Planet.

There they had been — Dr. and Mrs. Topman and Cap'n Tom — standing in a little group on the beach by the big black rock, the dazzling light of the early morning sun turning the ocean side of it golden. Excitedly the three had waved as the little space ship came plummeting onto the sand, then stood gazing upward as the fierce flames from the rocket exhausts ceased their roaring. There was a breath of silence, then Chuck flung open the door and looked down at them.

"Hi!" he called. And he grinned — a big, wide, mischievous grin.

"Young man," called up Cap'n Tom, but there was a twinkle in his eye if only Chuck could have seen it, "I have a small bone to pick with you." He meant, of course, Chuck's going off without asking him.

157

But Chuck only sat there with that maddening expression still on his face.

"We have a surprise for you," he said.

"Well, *what*, Chuck, *what?*" cried Mrs. Topman, who, womanlike, could not bear suspense and never made any attempt to put up with it. "Come down here at once and tell us. Where's David — he's all right, isn't he?"

"Oh, *he's* all right," replied Chuck, and leaped out onto the sand.

Inside the ship, David chuckled and winked at Ta, and just as the little man moved over to the door, David put his head out over Ta's shoulder and so caught the memorable flick of time when Mrs. Topman first glimpsed that strange, small face under the broad forehead.

Of course there could be no mistaking the fact that this was not Mr. Theo, and her mouth dropped open as she saw the necklace of big stones swing across the chest of the stranger, the large domed head and the semitransparent robes. She put one hand up to her throat and the other on Dr. Topman's arm as if to support herself.

As for Dr. Topman and Cap'n Tom, they seemed to lose their breaths entirely. They tried to speak but no sound came. "We are looking — we are actually *looking*," you could see them thinking, "at a being from another world."

"It's the Great Ta, Mom and Dad," shouted David, bursting with satisfaction and triumph. "He came with us, and brought Brumblium for Mr. Brumblydge. Golly, we're *starved* — what about breakfast, Mom? And what will you give His Majesty? We never thought about that. Do you suppose Dad could drive over to Mr. Bass's and get some mushrooms out of the cellar? Do you think you could, Dad?"

Dr. Topman nodded, but did not appear to be certain just what had been asked of him. Then he drew himself up, stepped forward and made a little courtly bow.

"Great Ta," he said, "please forgive the effect this unexpected happening has had on us. We do welcome you — believe me. In fact, we shall do everything we can to make you as comfortable and happy as possible. As for Mr. Brumblydge, he will be overjoyed to see you. You will do him all the good my medical science has failed to do."

At this fine speech of welcome, Ta smiled and stepped onto the threshold of the space ship's door, then gave a jump and seemed to float onto the sand like a bit of thistledown. There he stood — a pale,

but very definite green, not any taller than David or Chuck, wrapped about in those strange, pinkish, not quite transparent robes of his, the necklace of richly hued stones luminous as live things in the brilliant sunlight, and kingly from the crown of his almost bald head to the soles of his feet, which were shod in rather Grecian-looking sandals.

Mrs. Topman was plainly just able to get hold of herself.

"Your Majesty," and she put out her hand which Ta gravely and gently took in both his own in a quick gesture of friendliness, "David and Chuck have told us about you many times, but all they have said seemed like a dream to me. I know that they actually travel in space, that they have landed on your planet, and that Mr. Theo has gone there to live with your people. Tyco Bass comes and goes — he is in another galaxy, the boys tell me. And now *you* are here! Can you understand how I . . . ?"

Ta laughed, shaking his head, and it was clear that he was laughing at himself and not at her.

"David's mother, don't imagine you are the only one to feel as you do. In the last two hours I have lived a lifetime and, in the past half-hour, I have even discovered a new language in my mouth and an entirely new voice! Now, on top of everything else, I am in a new world and there, just as Theo described them, are the Moving Waters —" Here Ta looked out over that sparkling expanse of deep blue in which thousands of small waves raced forward and lost themselves in giant rollers. He stared up at the sky and his amazed eyes followed the airy flight of gulls and the low, level flight of cormorants. Then they went beyond, to where a little racing yacht, out for early practice, sped like a white butterfly, and beyond that to a tanker making its slow, patient way along the horizon. "You see," he said, "I find *this* almost impossible to believe."

A few minutes later, the space ship and its precious cargo of Brumblium was stored away in the cave until it could be unloaded. Then the party of six set off across the sand, Dr. Topman and Cap'n Tom going ahead, with Ta between them, and David and Mrs. Topman and Chuck coming along behind.

"But what shall I give him to *eat?*" Mrs. Topman was exclaiming under her breath to the two boys. "Oh, to think that I have a king on my hands, and not only a king but one from another planet! Really, David Topman, the things you do to your poor old parents are simply unspeakable. What if I should poison him? And what will the neighbors say when they see him — all green and in those peculiar robes?

162

It's too much, and Mr. Brumblydge still so sick! Of course, we *can* get mushrooms, but I'm almost certain he won't be able to eat meat or maybe anything else at all, and then —"

"Now, listen, Mom," interrupted David, "Chuck and I had a whole meal of mushrooms on Basidium, lots of different kinds, and we weren't sick a bit, so probably Ta won't get sick here —"

"Well, if he does," his mother said, "it will be the last straw. I shall go away and you boys will have to take over. I shall just give up." Then all at once she smiled to herself. "All the same," she added, "it *is* exciting. What other woman in the whole world has ever had an extraterrestrial being for a house guest, and a royal one at that?"

Prewytt, looking very weak and wan and as unlike his brisk, sturdy self as possible, was sitting up in bed having an eggnog. There was not the slightest hint of green left in his skin, which, of course, had he been well, there would have been. But when David and Chuck stuck their heads in at his bedroom door, a broad smile lit his face.

"Oh, boys! How glad I am to see you've got safely back! Mrs. Topman told me you took off for Basidium last night at midnight especially for me. Thank

163

you both — I am very grateful to you." Then his smile faded a little and an anxious, questioning look came into his brown eyes. He did not say it, but they knew he was wordlessly asking: had they got the Brumblium?

"Mr. Brumblydge, we have a visitor to see you," announced Chuck, his eyes shining with anticipation.

"You — you *have?*"

"Yes," said David, "and don't you worry, we got the Brumblium! In fact your visitor insisted on bringing it. Now he wants to have a good long talk with you if you feel up to it. Great Ta," and at these words Ta stepped in, "we should like to present to you one of the most famous scientists on the Great Protector, Mr. Prewytt Brumblydge. Mr. Brumblydge, here at last from fifty thousand miles away in space is His Majesty, the King of Basidium, the Mushroom Planet, who has come for an interview with you on a matter of the utmost importance." You could almost hear trumpets sounding, and bugles blowing, and a roll of drums the way David made that announcement.

Prewytt had started so violently at the words "Great Ta," that he had almost spilled his eggnog. Then he sl-o-w-ly put out his arm and, without look-

164

ing, his round eyes held as if hypnotized by the sight of his incredible visitor, he managed to set the glass down on the table beside his bed. Ta, his hand outstretched came across to him, and Dr. and Mrs. Topman and Cap'n Tom came in and stood smiling at the sight of a meeting which no one had ever imagined could take place in this room.

"I — I can't even get up, Your Majesty. But I am — oh, I am *greatly* honored. Forgive me — this stupid illness — please sit down —"

David put a chair near the bed, Ta took Prewytt's hand for a moment, then he settled himself, his robes faintly rustling, and a look of delight on his face at being in the presence of one he had come so far to see. As for Prewytt, sunk in his pillows as he was, all tucked up with a hot water bottle, the sleeves of Dr. Topman's pajamas falling over his hands, his collar twisted round and his hair standing up in peaks, he seemed to forget his embarrassed astonishment entirely. Perhaps it was Ta's easy naturalness, perhaps it was because Prewytt had thought of this moment ever since the desire had first come to him to fly to Basidium. But at any rate, those two were soon talking as though they had known one another all their lives, and Mrs. Topman beckoned the others to come away and leave them to themselves.

"They strike the same note exactly," she said, "which is what real friends usually do right from the beginning. Well, *that's* settled, and the awful question is now, what on earth am I to serve a Basidium-ite king for his breakfast?"

Ta, the King

A<small>LL</small> the while Ta was in the bedroom talking to Prewytt, and Dr. Topman was off at Thallo Street in the station wagon to get some fresh mushrooms from Mr. Bass's cellar, David and Chuck were getting underfoot in the kitchen. Certainly they could have waited to tell their story of the Lost City of Basidium until Dr. Topman got back, but what with Cap'n Tom sitting there bursting to hear it all and urging them on, and Mrs. Topman stopping every other minute to exclaim and ask questions, they simply could not keep it to themselves.

And when Dr. Topman returned, of course they had to begin all over again, with more details, and went on to how they had found Ta and Mr. Theo in the Hall of the Ancient Ones and described vividly the memorable scene of Ta's announcement back at the palace. It was really a marvel that Mrs. Topman was able to get any sort of meal together at all, but she finally did.

167

And just as they were about to ask Ta if he would like to come and have his breakfast, who should come charging out of the bedroom but Prewytt, leaving Ta standing in anxious concern at the door.

"I did try my best to keep him —" he began.

"Why, Mr. Brumblydge, you just get right back!" cried Mrs. Topman.

"Come now, old man, you're in no shape yet for that sort of thing," said Dr. Topman firmly. "Into bed with you at once."

But Prewytt didn't even hear them. His eyes were shining, his whole body was positively shooting off sparks of eagerness and enthusiasm. He no longer looked peaked and wan and pale. He seemed miraculously to have filled out a little, though it was perhaps Dr. Topman's baggy pajamas that gave the effect, the legs of which Prewytt had to hold up so that he could stride about in his impatience. His face had taken on color, and he appeared in every way to be his old assured, restless, indomitable self.

"My dear boys," he exclaimed, "how can I ever thank you for going to get the Brumblium for me! And to bring His Majesty here into the bargain! What a talk we have had! What a brain His Majesty has! And to think he has consented to stay while I build another Brumblitron, which I shall start immediately! And I have had the most marvelous idea!

168

Why not sell the rights to the Brumblitron to some large company, for a quite substantial sum of money, seeing as how I need money so badly? I can't imagine why I've never thought of this! Now, Mrs. Topman, if I could just have my suit —"

Well, it was all they could do to get him back into his bed. He had no job, he kept pleading. Even if Dr. Frobisher insisted that he go back to the San Julian Observatory, he would not do it after all that had happened. He simply would not put Horace Frobisher in the awful position of having to take him back out of kindness and friendship. And he really should pay Austin Shellworthy what it had cost him to have that fence put up — or he should pay part of the cost, anyway. Also he should have a pamphlet published, or call in the newspaper reporters at once, so as to explain just why he had buried the bones and to let it be known that he had *not* intended a trick or a hoax in any way whatsoever.

Of course David and Chuck were bursting to hear him talk more about this, but Dr. Topman insisted on getting Prewytt settled and quieted down. And he must have been exhausted with excitement, for in five minutes he was fast asleep — a beautiful, deep, peaceful sleep, such as he had not had since he'd first taken sick.

"Great Ta," began David eagerly when they were

169

all gathered round the big table in the dining room for breakfast, "*did* Mr. Brumblydge tell you why he buried the bones in the cliff when you were in there talking to him for so long? He's been too sick until now for any of us to ask him about it."

Ta shook his head. By this time he understood what had been going on in Pacific Grove and about Pacific Grove man, for the boys had told him everything that they knew on the way home in the space ship.

"No, he said nothing about it. All he spoke of — and I shall have to admit that Mr. Brumblydge did most of the talking — was about the Brumblitron and his Theory of the Universe, so that I would understand exactly why he needs Brumblium so badly. Now I understand about the earth's need for fresh water and how the Brumblitron can supply it, and how more research with this invention of his will help him to clear up many of the problems in his Theory." Here Ta paused for a moment, looking extremely thoughtful. "He said, you know, that until he completely understands the negative universe, he will never be able to come to any final conclusion."

"Great Ta, what *is* the negative universe?" asked David.

"Well, Mr. Brumblydge tells me," replied Ta, "that it is the invisible companion of this positive universe

170

we live in. And he said that just as our universe is made up of the plain, ordinary matter we are so familiar with, so the negative universe is made up of anti-matter. He said that earth scientists know, from certain experiments they've made, that this anti-matter actually does exist, because they've *seen* particles of anti-matter destroy particles of ordinary matter. Think of that! Oh, I'm certain your Prewytt Brumblydge won't rest until he has explored this mysterious realm in some way or another —"

"*Explored!*" burst out Chuck. "Well, *how* —"

But just then, in came Mrs. Topman with a casserole of cheese soufflé, all puffed up and dark golden. There was a bowl of mushrooms browned in butter to go with it, for those who liked mushrooms. There was crisp bacon (Ta had five slices), and hot muffins of a melting lightness (six of these, well spread with butter and strawberry jam, disappeared from his plate).

David watched Ta tucking away all this food with astonishment and some anxiety, but His Majesty seemed to be in the highest spirits. And when he told Mrs. Topman with enthusiasm that this was the most delicious meal he'd ever had in his life, she glowed.

"Thank you, Your Highness. I've never been complimented by a king on my cooking, and I must say I like it."

The moment they were finished, Chuck jumped up from the table.

"Now," he said, "we can take His Majesty downtown and show him all the sights. Want to come, Grandpop — and you, Dr. Topman?"

But Dr. Topman said that he must start out at once to call on his patients. However, just as he was going out the front door, Cap'n Tom called after him:

"Keep an eye peeled, Frank — see how many Mycetians you can spot. They seem to be all over the place for some reason or other. Maybe you can find out why."

"Mycetians!" exclaimed David.

"Here in Pacific Grove?" Chuck asked.

"You mean a whole lot of them, Tom?" And Dr. Topman came back in again.

"Yep," said Cap'n Tom, giving his crisp, white hair a quick ruffle. "I was down on the wharf in Monterey last night — that was where I was when you people were hunting for me to ask about Chuck's taking-off — and when I was on the way home, it gradually began to dawn on me that they were everywhere — in Monterey *and* Pacific Grove. And different nationalities! Little Welsh ones, English ones, Swedish, French, Italian — and all very, very pale green, though the color's not so noticeable at night. But besides being small, they did look different, no doubt of that. Whole families there were, deep in discussion about something, and some awfully solemn little men in groups. I tell you, what with their heads nod-

ding and bobbing, they looked just about as earnest and learned as you can imagine."

"Perhaps a Mycetian gathering, for some secret purpose," ventured Ta.

"Yes, but why here, and what are they up to, do you suppose?" wondered Mrs. Topman.

Everybody looked at everybody else with the same uneasy glance, and it seemed to David that they were all having the same suspicions. But now, just as they were standing there, a listening look suddenly came into Cap'n Tom's round, weather-beaten face, and his blue eyes grew sharp.

"Whish-sht!" he said, and his hand came to his mouth.

Everybody quieted. And what they heard was a kind of subdued confusion, a far-off uproar, with occasional high notes shooting out of it and, underneath, a low, steady thudding.

"Well, now, what's *that?*" demanded Dr. Topman. "It sounds like a parade. But why would a parade be coming clear out here near the ocean?"

So now they all went to the front porch and when they came into the open they could tell at once that there was a commotion around the corner a couple of blocks away. Shouts could be heard. People began coming out of their houses all up and down Frigate

174

Way, to crane their necks, and a few began running along the street toward the corner to get a good view. Then David heard it again — a deep *b-oo-mm-m, b-oo-mm-m, b-oo-mpity, b-oo-mpity, boo-m-m.* It sounded like a big bass drum. *B-oo-m-mm, b-oo-m-mm* — and there it came around the corner onto Frigate, and it *was* a big bass drum, right in the middle of the street.

With it was a sturdy, thickly-built little Mycetian who had it on straps around his shoulders and who was beating it. He looked very pleased with himself, as well he might, for he was crossing over hands, throwing the drumsticks into the air, and turning around every now and then and walking backwards so that he could grin at the whole crowd of Mycetians who were following along after him.

Well, *he* wasn't so bad, though David thought his expression of self-satisfaction was pretty sickening. It was those six others right behind him who were carrying long strips of heavy paper, the ends of which were attached to poles, with a Mycetian holding each pole. One strip said in enormous black letters:

DOWN WITH PREWYTT BRUMBLYDGE

Another read:

THE TRICKSTER MUST BE TRIED!

And a third proclaimed:

P. BRUMBLYDGE IS NO LONGER
ONE OF US!

Behind them flowed the crowd, bulging over the street onto the sidewalks and lawns.

"— the rougher element, by jings," David heard Cap'n Tom mutter under his breath, "and headed straight for this house —"

The minute David read those signs, a flash of blazing anger at the rank injustice of calling Mr. Brumblydge a trickster shot through him, and without a word he made for the street with Chuck at his heels. And they threw themselves onto the banner carriers and the drum beater.

After that, nobody could have told exactly what happened. Shouts went up. Everybody milled around. Cap'n Tom and Dr. Topman charged forward trying to separate the boys from the Mycetians, but David and Chuck were too quick and furious for them. Down came the banners, and the drumsticks went flying, though how two boys could have accomplished so much in so short a time is still a puzzle.

By now the drum beater and the banner carriers were dancing with indignation, and the crowd of

Mycetians was boiling around Dr. Topman and Cap'n Tom and the boys so that they must have been completely lost to view. Because all at once David was dimly aware that his mother was calling out in terror.

"David! David! Chuck! Where are you? Please — help, someone — get the —"

And then a most astonishing thing happened.

"SILENCE!" came a deep voice.

And there *was* silence. The tangle of arms and legs became untangled. Everyone straightened and turned. And when David looked up, there was Ta on the porch standing beside his mother.

Ta was not quite as tall as Mrs. Topman but you could not take your eyes from him. He seemed, by some unmistakable authority in his bearing, by some powerful magnetism, to command attention. His strange, pinkish beige robes were, without a doubt, the robes of royalty. His large head with its broad, high dome needed no crown, for a crown was invisibly there. And his large, piercing, dark eyes seemed to root that disorderly throng to the spot.

Without a word he stood there, and his gaze swept back and forth across all those faces. Some eyes could not meet his but slid down or away to the side and crept back to his face only when they no longer needed to take that awful concentration full on.

Now, when complete silence reigned, Ta made an imperious, beckoning gesture with both arms and the crowd drew near.

"*Shame!*" he said at last — that single word. "I feel deep *shame* for each one of you." He studied them. "You, who are Mycetians, who are Spore People, have done this cheap and stupid thing. You have formed yourselves into an unthinking mob so that you act like a single animal ruled by its instincts. And why? To cast forth one of your own race, to vent your resentment upon him when you have not heard a single word of his own story. Do you *know* that he has played a trick? Do you *know* that he is guilty of any wrongdoing at all? *Do you?*" demanded Ta in a terrible voice.

Silence. Then a faint whispering, a murmuring, a muttering.

"No," David heard. "No — but we read — someone said — we were told —"

"Someone said! You were told! You read somewhere! But what facts have been presented? What do you know of Prewytt Brumblydge's side of the matter? What men, who are capable of judging, have heard his side of the matter? What has been proved? Nothing. Nothing has been heard or judged or proved. Therefore, you will disband at once. You will disperse and make no more scenes — humiliating for yourselves as well as the rest of your race who value the dignity and honor of the Mycetians more than you do, it would seem, but who value the truth above all else.

"Now *go!*"

And all those little, pale green people, after staring a moment longer into the stern face of Ta, the King, turned and went quietly away. Five minutes later there was not a sign that they had ever been there; not a torn banner, not a broken pole remained. For a minute or two, the neighbors seemed to hesitate on the verge of coming to the Topmans' in order to discuss in amazed wonder this whole sudden surging up of events. But something, apparently, made them think the better of it, for they whispered in groups for a little and then they too disappeared.

In the house, Ta stood at the window of the Topmans' living room staring out over the sea, and the others (except for Dr. Topman who had finally had to depart on his calls) waited for him to speak.

"What an astonishing thing it is," he said at last, "that here on this planet the earthen Basidiumites — the Mycetians — should feel themselves to be my people too. Do you think that I presumed, my friends?" and here he turned to them, to Mrs. Topman and Cap'n Tom and David and Chuck. "I am your guest — and I have spoken as if I were not a

179

guest. But when I saw what was happening, it was as if another voice than mine came from my lips — and yet, at the same time, those *were* my people!"

"Your Majesty, it seems to me that they are certainly your people," said Annabelle Topman, "and who could question what you did? All we can do is to offer you our thanks, because I don't know what would have happened if it hadn't been for you. But that *was* strange, the way they looked at you — the power you seemed to have over them — the respect they had for you — someone they'd never seen before in their lives!"

"Well, one thing's certain," said David, and he was still a bit shaken from what he and Chuck had just been through, "they recognized you, Great Ta, even if they didn't have any idea who you are. Maybe it's in their blood, somehow, to recognize a member of the royal Basidiumites. Maybe it'll never die out as long as the race of spore people lasts."

How could it be, David had asked Mr. Bass once, that one branch of the race should live here on earth and another branch on that little globe thousands of miles distant in space? And Mr. Bass had answered that perhaps a seed of life, a tiny spore, had landed on Basidium in the far, far distant past in the heart of a meteor, and another spore-bearing meteor had darted through our atmosphere to earth. But whether

180

the Lost Planet, whose fragments are the asteroids between Mars and Jupiter, was the parent world from which the meteors might have come, even Mr. Bass did not know.

Now Chuck, who had picked up the morning paper from a corner of the porch, held it out so that they could all see the headline:

MYCETIANS MUM ON REASON FOR PENINSULA VISIT

"Ah," said Cap'n Tom, taking the paper from Chuck, "so! I have a feeling that now everything is about to come to a head."

Which it was, for just then there came three sharp raps at the front door.

CHAPTER 20

Prewytt Refuses

DAVID tore down the hall, and the instant he opened the door, and saw those eight short, solemn, dark-haired, bushy-eyebrowed, large-headed, exceedingly Mycetian-looking gentlemen standing waiting with their hats in their hands, he was certain they had something to do with the League.

"Yes, sir?" said David to the one who seemed to be in charge because he was standing in front.

"Would this be the Topman residence?" inquired the little man in soft, musical tones, his thick, standing-out eyebrows going right up. At the same time all the other pairs of eyebrows went up.

Now Annabelle Topman came forward.

"I am Mrs. Topman," she said. "Is there something I can do for you?"

"Mistress Topman," he returned politely, and his eyebrows came down again, "I am Towyn Niog, and this is Mistar Selwyn Llandovery, Mistar Llewellyn Jones, Mistar Ellis Cwymawynn, Mistar Rhys

182

Colwyn, Mistar Mostyn Rhyl, Mistar Hue Ebbyn, and Mistar Davies Machynleith. There is serious purpose we have in coming here, Mistress Topman, for it is the Mycetian League we are — at least in part — and we would speak with a certain guest of yours, Mistar Prewytt Brumblydge."

Annabelle Topman drew in her breath, and a wary, protective look crept into her face.

"The Mycetian League!" she repeated. "Oh, but I am afraid that Mr. Brumblydge is *very* ill, gentlemen, far, far too ill to be able to —"

But, would you believe it — just as she spoke these words, there came floating along the hall, from behind that closed door on the other side of the living room, an unmistakably happy, tenor, Welsh voice raised in unmistakable Welsh song:

> "Under yonder oaken tree
> Whose branches oft me shaded;
> Elves and fairies dance with glee
> When day's last beams hath faded:
> Then while the stars shine brightly,
> So airy, gay and sprightly,
> 'Till Chanticleer tells dawn is here,
> They trip it, trip it lightly —"

"Ah!" breathed Towyn Niog as the last word wafted gently away. "What a lovely voice it is — long have I known that song. There is astonishing

183

how one man should be blessed with such a voice, as well as the intellect of genius to probe the heavens and form all sorts of new ideas about it. And he is ill, you say."

"Oh, but, Mr. Niog," burst out David, "Mr. Brumblydge always sings in his fever — and recites poetry, too —"

"*Well!*" returned Mr. Niog. "Well, now, I shall leave this communication with you, then, Mistress Topman" — and he handed her a long, legal-looking envelope — "to be passed on to Mistar Brumblydge whenever you think he shall feel able to read it. I do hope, for his sake, that that will be soon." He bent upon her a considering gaze.

"Mr. Niog, won't you and the other gentlemen come in?" said Mrs. Topman, and David could tell that his mother was horribly embarrassed. "Perhaps I might just see if Mr. Brumblydge —"

"No need," returned Towyn, holding up a faintly green hand. "Thank you, but no need at all. Good day to you, Mistress Topman, and to you, young sir."

"Good day," murmured all the other little Welsh gentlemen. "Good day." And they turned and filed solemnly down the steps, along the walk, and over to a car that stood at the curb. Into it they stowed themselves, quickly and neatly, and zoomed off.

At once, with set lips and flashing eyes (David shivered, for he had known that fire flash at *him*), Mrs. Topman turned and marched along the hall, past Chuck, and into the living room where Ta and Cap'n Tom stood waiting.

"The Mycetian League, Mr. Brumblydge," she called out, and there was an edge to her voice and her cheeks were bright pink. "*They heard!*" She rapped smartly upon his door.

"Got it! Got it! Got it!" came caroling from within, which meant Prewytt hadn't heard a word she said. "Mrs. Topman, dear, *would* you believe it — !" And the door of the bedroom burst open and Prewytt stood there beaming with triumph, his pajama pants hiked up under his arms, his hands full of papers, and a pencil stuck behind his ear. "Oh, my goodness," he exclaimed, taking in their serious faces, "what's the matter?"

"I *said* that the Mycetian League has been here, Mr. Brumblydge," returned Annabelle Topman. "They left you this."

At once the light of happy triumph died from Prewytt's face (he had no doubt conquered at last some knotty problem of his Theory of the Universe). He took the envelope and opened it and, while

everyone looked on with held breath, glanced over the enclosed pages, which crackled richly, and then turned and got back into bed.

"I think," he said with curious quietness, "that you had better hear." So they all gathered round, and Prewytt began to read. "This is a decree," he explained, "issued by the Mycetian League from Llanbedr in Wales, to Prewytt M. Brumblydge of San Julian, California.

"ITEM 1: *Whereas* Prewytt M. Brumblydge, having, against the Ancient Laws and Dictates of his people, kept hidden among his own possessions the bones of his ancestors, whose one and rightful resting place is known to all Mycetians, and

"ITEM 2: *Whereas* Mr. Brumblydge, instead of returning the aforesaid bones to the aforesaid resting place, did bury them in such a way and in such a location as to result in a most ludicrous and shameful trick being played upon the entire world of science, and

"ITEM 3: *Whereas* this action of Mr. Brumblydge's has caused the disruption of work as well as great and unnecessary expense of time, energy and money to Dr. Austin Shellworthy as well as to many other prominent individuals whose time could have been better employed than in traveling across the country to no purpose, and

"ITEM 4: *Whereas* this action caused the failure

of advancement in position to one Dr. Ambrose Mellander Bullen, as well as humiliation to him because of the stand he had taken, and

"ITEM 5: *Whereas* this action is causing disrepute and suspicion to fall upon the work of the San Julian Observatory, with which Mr. Brumblydge is associated, so that the research and conclusions of its astronomers shall henceforth be connected to their embarrassment with what is unfortunately known as the Great Brumblydge Hoax,

"*Therefore* we, the undersigned members of the Mycetian League, do ordain and declare that Prewytt M. Brumblydge shall stand trial before us two weeks from the date of delivery of this decree, and at an hour and place of our choosing, at which time Mr. Brumblydge shall respectfully and truthfully make known to us the reasons for his action, whether or not his action was meant as a hoax or trick upon some one person, or upon the world of science in general, and finally whether he himself deliberately removed the aforesaid bones from their rightful resting place.

"*Be it known that* Mr. Brumblydge shall not discuss this matter with any save those persons who are directly concerned and whose help or advice is needed, and

"*Be it known that* Mr. Brumblydge shall immediately, before the trial, return the bones to their rightful resting place, or if this is not possible, directly after the trial.

Signed, TOWYN NIOG, etc. etc."

Prewytt looked up from the pages he held and his large, brown eyes burned.

"I'll not do it!" he cried, and down came his fist on his knee poked up under the blanket. "I'll not do it — go like a craven, superstitious coward and put those bones back. What difference does it make where the bones rest? The person who owned them has been dead these five hundred thousand years! They're priceless where they are, in the hands of the anthropologists who are studying them. Let them stay there. I'll not move them."

"And we cannot persuade you otherwise, is that it, my friend?" asked Ta in a low voice.

"No, Your Majesty. The decision is up to me. If I am wrong, I shall suffer the consequences."

Later, when David and Chuck were alone with Mr. Brumblydge, David got his jacket and pulled from the pocket that old daguerreotype with the label on the back saying, "Morgan Caerwen and Prewytt M. Brumblydge, October 15, 1832."

"Mr. Brumblydge," he said, holding it out to him where he sat huddled among his pillows with his arms locked round his knees, "when I came in to see you just before Chuck and I took off for Basidium, I found this photograph lying on the floor where your jacket had been hanging. I shouldn't

189

have taken it, but I did — to show Chuck. And here it is back. But could you tell us, Mr. Brumblydge, is *this* Prewytt M. Brumblydge your grandfather, your great-grandfather, or your great-great-grandfather — or who?"

Prewytt stared at the photograph for some time, but almost as though he scarcely saw it. Then he took it and put it under his pillow.

"Thank you, David. I shall need that photograph. And I must write to my Aunt Matilda Brumblydge at once to come for the trial. Because I shall need her too."

A Matter of Pride

THE trial, Prewytt was finally told, was to be held at the place where Dr. Shellworthy had given his talk on that fateful evening of Prewytt's return: the library of SAGA Hall. It would commence, he was told, at nine sharp in the morning.

Once again the tables were cleared away and dozens of folding chairs were put in. Everyone arrived early, so that by the time Ta and the Topmans, Cap'n Tom and the boys and Mr. Brumblydge came into the paneled room with the tall windows and the rows and rows of books, it was already filled with a sea of small, pale green Mycetian faces. And what a sight it was to see them all gathered together in one room!

Ta, of course, caused a tremendous stir when he entered in his long robes and with that air of calm dignity which he wore with such naturalness. He walked down the center aisle with an easy stride that sent the necklace of rich Basidiumite jewels swinging across his chest. At sight of him, all the Mycetians rose. At once, Towyn Niog, who had been seated at a large table at the front of the room, got up and came to him and bowed. There were a few murmured words between them, and also with Prewytt Brumblydge. Then Ta turned to Mrs. Topman and excused himself, and Towyn Niog led him forward to one of two imposing chairs which had been placed at the center of that large table facing the room.

Prewytt followed and went to a chair which had been placed to the right on the opposite side of the table near the audience. Now all the members of the League began coming in and seating themselves to the right and left of those two big central chairs. As well as Towyn Niog and his seven companions of the other day, there were now four more, which made twelve.

"But, Dave," whispered Chuck, when they had found seats up near Dr. Shellworthy, "I thought there were thirteen members in the League — oh, of course — Mr. Bass is missing —"

"— so I guess he won't get here after all," returned David, bitterly disappointed. "I was hoping —"

But just then the door behind Towyn Niog opened, the members of the League turned expectantly, and there stood —

"Mr. Bass!" shouted David and Chuck together, springing up out of their seats and making a horrible, loud clatter with their feet.

"Sh-shh-shh!" hissed everybody, craning their necks to stare at the two boys, but Dr. Shellworthy smiled and put his hand on David's arm and pulled him down.

Oh, how different Mr. Bass looked, somehow, thought David. How remote he seemed, terribly solemn, and, what was worst of all, he no longer had his gardening coat on but an unfamiliar jacket David could not remember having seen him in before. At the sound of the boys calling his name, his face brightened for an instant and he turned and smiled at them. Then he took his place in that one remaining big chair in the very center, the one next to Ta, spoke to him in low tones, bent upon Prewytt a grave and searching look, and now — lifted the gavel!

"Dave, *Mr. Bass is the judge —*"

Well, of course, David said to himself. Who else? And it seemed perfectly natural to him, but also a sign of the extreme honor in which Mr. Bass was held by the League, that they should trust him to judge at the trial of his own friend.

But just as Mr. Bass had brought down the gavel — bang! — there came a commotion outside the

193

closed and locked door of the trial chamber. A high, indignant female voice was heard to protest violently, a clacketing as of some hard, metallic, pointed instrument was heard upon the paneling of the door until it was finally opened and in burst a little old lady brandishing a long, tightly rolled umbrella.

"Your Honor," cried the poor Mycetian who had been posted at the door to keep intruders away, "I know it's after nine, and I *tried* —"

"It is all right," replied Mr. Bass in a clear voice. "Come, Miss Brumblydge, please be seated at once."

Whereupon Aunt Matilda, with snapping brown eyes and a spot of faint green in each cheek, sailed down the center aisle. She had on a neat little traveling suit, kid gloves, and a small, veiled hat perched right on top of her upswept, shining white hair. She had a round face and firm, round figure, which was not in the least fat. When she saw that there was an empty seat in the very first row in front of Cap'n Tom, she took it, settling herself with a quick, bustling flurry.

"Trying to keep me out of the trial of my own nephew!" she whispered loudly to the woman next to her. "Young men are so bossy these days. I *never* —"

Bang! went Mr. Bass's gavel. Mr. Brumblydge

194

sent his Aunt Matilda a quick, questioning glance — and the trial began.

"Mr. Towyn Niog will first read out the charges against the defendant, Mr. Prewytt M. Brumblydge," came Tyco's clear, carrying voice, which had a tone in it David had never heard before.

So now the words of Mr. Niog rang sternly through the long, high-ceilinged room where the autumn sunlight slanted palely as if in an effort to cheer things up a bit. And his voice seemed to make the charges much worse than when Prewytt himself had read them out in the bedroom at home. All the way through, Aunt Matilda could be heard exclaiming under her breath, "Oh, imagine! . . . Isn't it awful! . . . I tried to tell him! . . . He never was one to pay any heed . . . Just listen to that!"

And when the list was finished . . .

"Prewytt Brumblydge," spoke Mr. Bass, "have you, by this time" — and he leaned forward, and there seemed to David to be a strong note of concern in his voice — "returned the bones in question to their rightful resting place as was suggested to you in the Decree?"

"No, Your Honor," replied Prewytt firmly, "and I might as well make it clear here and now that I do not *ever intend* returning the bones to that resting place —"

"*Oh-h-h-h!*" swept over the whole room, a sigh of horror.

"— because if I did, Your Honor, how could I truly say to myself that I hadn't done it out of fear of Wyrd? Do you imagine for a moment that I believe in Wyrd and all that hocus-pocus about 'blackest misfortune'? I am a scientist, Your Honor, as you are yourself, not one of your old wives mumbling rubbish in a chimney corner."

Pock! went twelve pens into twelve inkwells, and *scritch, scratch, scritch, scratch, scritch* they went across the pages of twelve ledgers.

"I see," said Tyco Bass gravely. "Then will you, Mr. Brumblydge, tell us your story from the beginning: how you acquired the bones, why you have kept them with you, and why you buried them where you did."

Prewytt looked off and away through the long window opposite him, but he did not seem to see the light and shadow moving beyond.

"Great Ta, Your Honor, and gentlemen of the Mycetian League, permit me to begin with the burial — or rather with a blowout, for that, I think, is the real beginning.

"You see, it happened upon a road high above the ocean near Austin Shellworthy's home — a blowout that appeared to me at the time to be the latest in a whole series of narrow escapes and misfortunes. For brevity's sake, I shall name only four.

"Among the first of those that have happened lately was the incident of my amazing invention, the Electronic Telescope Filter, which I dropped and smashed to pieces on the floor of the San Julian Observatory, and which I have never been able to duplicate since. Clamped upon the eyepiece of the telescope, it opened up wonders of outer space which astronomers of earth have only dreamed of. But though I could swear I put down every step in the process of creating it, one of those steps I must have failed to record and it is now apparently lost to me forever.

"Next came the incident of my first Brumblitron which, had I not cast it into the sea at the critical moment, would have exploded and taken not only my own life, but the lives of two very dear friends of mine as well.

"Shortly afterwards, there was the incident of the yawning chasm into which I fell and almost drowned when the sea came plunging and roaring in through a subterranean cavern. How I saved myself is a miracle — but again I almost lost my life.

"Finally, gentlemen, there was the incident of the blowout. So violently and suddenly did my car swerve that it came within a hair's breadth of plung-

197

ing over the side of a steep ravine. As it was, the front wheel halted at the ravine's very edge and, had it gone an inch further, I would have been lost.

"It was this third narrow escape that seemed to me to be the last straw. I began to be frightened. Lack of enough sleep, no doubt, and the fact that I was coming down with influenza, brought about my defeat. I remembered that verse about Wyrd and blackest misfortune. And it was then, on that road near Austin Shellworthy's, that I decided to get rid of the bones, which I suspected, in this moment of weakness and soft-headedness, must be the cause of my misfortunes. I decided to give them to Austin Shellworthy.

"No, no, gentlemen of the League. Do not draw your brows down into those stern lines. For in the very next instant I knew that I could not give them to him, thus causing him in turn to be dogged by the ill fortune that had followed and almost killed me.

"Now came the fatal moment.

"Not long before this I had asked Dr. Frobisher to send down to me from San Julian a small seaman's chest which contained, among many important papers of mine, the box of bones. Unluckily, I had this chest with me in the trunk of my car, so that instead of repairing the blowout at once as I had intended to do, I got out that box.

"Looking about me, I spied a cliff at the foot of Austin Shellworthy's garden. And because I wanted those bones never to be seen again, never to be dug up by any living soul who might be hounded and threatened by death and bad luck as I had been, I decided to bury them there — *in* the cliff — *not* in the ground.

"But, gentlemen, no sooner had I entered the grove of oaks that shades and partially hides the cliff, than a most curious thing happened. A shiver went over me, as though a cold wind had blown down, and I saw a face out of the past — the far, faraway past. And I heard someone speak, just as clearly as you now hear me.

"That face was the face of my old professor, and I was sitting at his bedside. 'Treasure the bones with your life, Prewytt,' he said." And now Prewytt lifted his hand, and his voice took on the frail, high tones of a very old man. " 'Promise me to tell others what I have said — that the bones prove — that human creatures are very old, Prewytt, older by thousands and thousands of years than anyone has yet dreamed possible. They won't believe you — but you must be patient and prove to them step by step what I have taught you. It is all there in my notebook — and tell them — tell them —' and then his voice stopped, and his eyes changed, and I knew that he was dead.

"After that, I went all over Great Britain trying to explain what my old professor believed was the truth. But the bones and the notebook were handed back to me with smiles of amusement, and I was assured that the bones were only those of a young ape. What was worse, the fact that they glowed in the dark made everyone suspect that I had treated them with chemicals for a joke.

"Now, in disgust, I determined to come to America. But just before I left, I happened to tell my aunt that it was from the Mycetian graveyard at the top of the hundreds of stone steps near Llanbedr that I had gotten the bones. She was absolutely terrified, and even more so when I said that I had actually shown my old professor the way there, that he was a human being and not a Mycetian, and that we had discovered and dug the bones up together —"

Again a murmur of horror swept over that assemblage of small green faces. Eyes widened, everyone turned to everyone else, and *pock!* went the twelve pen-points into the twelve inkwells and *scritch, scratch, scritch, scratch, scritch* they went across the pages of the twelve ledgers. With an *ex-*
200

tremely serious face, Ta leaned over to say something into Tyco's ear. Towyn Niog's thick, standing-out eyebrows came down and met in one solid streak of blackness above his piercing dark eyes and the bridge of his nose, and *he* leaned over and said something into Tyco's other ear.

"Oh, golly, Chuck," breathed David, "what d'you suppose they'll do to Mr. Brumblydge?"

"It was at that time," went on Prewytt, without a quiver, as though he were not in the least aware of the effect of his words, "that my aunt repeated the rune to me and begged me to take the bones back to the graveyard. But I told her that as a scientist, I simply could not do anything so mindless and superstitious. In fact I told her that I was determined to keep the bones *precisely to prove the rune wrong!*"

Oh! *Pock!* More scritchings!

"So then," continued Prewytt, paying absolutely no attention, "to return to the present: I buried those three bones in the side of Austin Shellworthy's cliff and, having finished, I left and returned to Thallo Street.

"But now there occurred several things that combined to result in disaster for everyone: to begin with, my illness and a violent rainstorm out-of-season.

201.

"For if, gentlemen of the League, I had not become ill with influenza that very afternoon and gone up to my boardinghouse near the San Julian Observatory and stayed there in my own room without news or conversation of any sort for almost two weeks, I would have heard of Pacific Grove man and been able to explain him.

"And if it had not been for the rainstorm rushing down the face of the cliff in such a torrent that two of the bones were washed out and one remained visible to be dug out by Chuck Masterson and David Topman, this whole thing would never have happened.

"The third misfortune, of course, was that I made one small, tragic error in my own private method of fossil-dating. The bones were not 5000 years old as I had thought, but 500,000 years old. And if I had only known, I do not think I could have kept myself from taking them directly to Dr. Shellworthy and telling him how, after all, my old professor was proved right, years and years ahead of his time.

"Thus you can see, gentlemen of the League, how everything conspired against me. But not because of the rune, believe me. Quite the contrary! For don't you see that all this happened pre-*cise*ly because I deserted my stand as a scientist and consented to believe for a very short time that perhaps

202

that rune *did* cast a long, long shadow and that Wyrd had given the bones power over my life?

"So there you have it. This is the truth of the matter, gentlemen, and the end of my story as to why I acted as I did."

Now Towyn Niog whispered something to Mr. Bass, who nodded, and then Towyn leaned forward across the table, his dark brows again drawn severely together.

"Mistar Brumblydge," he said, "Dr. Austin Shellworthy himself has told me that thirty years ago — even forty years ago (and you cannot be over fifty or sixty now, at the very *most*) science was well along in its study of evolution. It would have been fascinated by your discovery, and I cannot believe that the outstanding men of anthropology in Great Britain would have mistaken those bones for an ape's — not in 1920 or thereabouts."

"But it was not 1920, Mr. Niog," replied Prewytt in a low voice.

"Ah! Well, when was it, then?"

Prewytt turned to Mr. Bass.

"Your Honor, I am not free to speak. This matter concerns someone beside myself and the person in question would have to come forward and give me permission to reveal just when it was."

Now the eyes of Ta, of Tyco, of Towyn Niog and

of the other eleven members of the League swept the courtroom. There was a tense silence. But not a soul moved or spoke.

"Plainly the person is unwilling to come forward, Mistar Brumblydge,," said Towyn, his eyes returning to Prewytt. "But what are we to make of your story if you refuse to give us proof of the one thing that is most important?"

Prewytt did not answer, but only stared at the floor. And then — who should get up but Aunt Matilda Brumblydge.

"Mr. Tyco Bass, Your Honor, it is my fault Prewytt is not speaking. He is keeping his promise to me, but I cannot bear that you should think he isn't telling the truth. Prewytt, *show* them the photograph! I have been a foolish old woman, and what they're about to find out doesn't really matter."

At this Prewytt drew from his coat pocket the daguerreotype that David had returned to him.

"Thank you, Aunt Matilda," he said, and his eyes were twinkling. "You are right, it doesn't matter. We neither of us, I think, look our ages." With these words he went over and laid the photograph down in front of Tyco Bass. "This, Great Ta and gentlemen of the League, shows me with my old professor, Dr. Morgan Caerwen, at the time of our discovery of the bones."

204

Ta and Tyco only smiled to themselves and nodded as they studied the picture and turned it over and saw the names and the date on the back. But as the other members of the League took the daguerreotype and read what was written, their eyes opened wide and their eyebrows went up and down like grasshoppers. They stared in awe at Prewytt, back at the photograph, and then up at Prewytt again. After that, something else dawned on them, and they stared even more appalled at poor Aunt Matilda.

"There can be no mistake, can there, gentlemen?" solemnly inquired Tyco Bass at length.

"No, no — there cannot, Your Honor," agreed Towyn Niog falteringly. "He is one of the Old Ones of our race, one of the *extremely rare* Old Ones. As for his aunt, Miss — ah, well — hmmph! Miss Brumblydge," he said, addressing her with enormous respect, "I must now beg your pardon, for it is the law among us that we must make known to all the nature of whatever exhibits we have in a case. So be it, then: Exhibit A," and here Towyn took up a stamp and went bang! on a pad, and bang! bang! on a big envelope into which he put Exhibit A, wrote on it, and then read out for everyone to hear, "Photograph of Prewytt M. Brumblydge, the defendant, and Dr. Morgan Caerwen, taken October 15, 1832."

205

At this statement, what a commotion arose in the court. Cries of "*1832!*" shot up from all over the room and one thoughtless, silly woman exclaimed, "Why, *he's* about one hundred and fifty years old, then, so that makes *her . . . !*" But everyone said, "*Sssshhhh!*" and David saw that Aunt Matilda's neck and the side of her face nearest him had lost its faint touch of green and gone absolutely white. But she did not

look to right or left but simply sat there, head up, resting her folded hands upon the handle of her umbrella.

Then Prewytt gave old Morgan Caerwen's notebook to Towyn, who marked it "Exhibit B," and now Tyco Bass, a look of concern on his kindly little face, turned to Prewytt again.

"Mr. Brumblydge, you have answered the court on accusation number one, as to why you did not return the bones to the Mycetian graveyard, and

on accusation number two, which concerns your reason for burying the bones. Will you speak next, please, on accusations three, four and five? What do you intend to do about the expense of time, energy and money which you have caused your friend, Dr. Austin Shellworthy?"

Prewytt turned and looked at Dr. Shellworthy and then back at Tyco.

"Your Honor, I can never return to Dr. Shellworthy the time and energy I unwittingly took from him. But I am more than anxious to return to him every penny he spent because of what I did. And I want him to know that —"

But at this moment Dr. Shellworthy got up.

"Your Honor, may I speak?" Tyco nodded. "I want it to be known, gentlemen of the League, that I would not take anything from Mr. Brumblydge. There is no need. For years I have been meaning to have just such a fence put up around my property. Now I have it, and it is a good fence, so why should anyone else pay for it? Other than this, I did not spend a cent. And if Mr. Brumblydge wishes to repay me for the time and energy I've spent over this astonishing turn of events, he has already done so. Never, in all my life, have I come across a subject that intrigues me more than the Mycetians. And if I may ask Prewytt Brumblydge, the Mycetian, endless questions in the future, I shall be in his debt, for I intend to write a book on the history and anthropology of his race."

With these words Austin Shellworthy sat down,

and a pleased smile broke across Prewytt's round face.

"I believe, Your Honor, that Dr. Shellworthy and I are about to have some intensely interesting conversations. That is," he added, in a funny, quizzical way, "unless I am otherwise occupied because of my misdoings.

"As for Dr. Ambrose Mellander Bullen," he went on, "no one asked him to come to Pacific Grove, nor to take the stand he did about the discovery. I do not feel in the least responsible for his scientific opinions. As for his failure to get the position he wanted," said Prewytt with a glint in his eye and what sounded like rather a wicked chuckle, "it turns out that my act did *not* cost him his advancement. Dr. Shellworthy wrote to the university, and they answered that they had decided several days *before* the news of the discovery came out that they would not offer Dr. Bullen their Chair of Anthropology."

Here Dr. Shellworthy went up with the university's letter and Towyn Niog went bang! bang! with his stamp and it was put with the other items as Exhibit C.

"But I can do nothing, Your Honor," Prewytt continued, "about the San Julian Observatory, except to resign from it, and I have offered to do this. Dr. Horace Frobisher, however, refuses to let me, and it

209

seems the other astronomers there feel the same way. Here is a letter from them which I shall always treasure, but I will loan it to you for a while as one of your exhibits."

Towyn nodded, took it, and stamped it "Exhibit D." And this might have seemed to finish things. Everyone heaved a sigh, but once more the tireless Towyn leaned forward.

"May I put one more question to the defendant, Your Honor?" Tyco nodded. "Mistar Brumblydge, is it not true that during your very first experiments on your Brumblitron in a certain place which you thought to be isolated, you gravely endangered the lives of those two boys, David Topman and Chuck Masterson, whom you have called your 'two very dear friends'? In fact, you said yourself that if you hadn't cast the Brumblitron into the sea, you would all have lost your lives."

At this Chuck leaped up, and right after him, David.

"Mr. Brumblydge didn't *ask* us to go there, Mr. Niog," Chuck declared. "Mr. Brumblydge didn't even *know* we were there —"

"And if he *had* known," David interrupted, "he'd never have started the experiment. Mr. Brumblydge wouldn't endanger *anybody's* life!"

"Ah, but the fact remains," replied Towyn Niog

fatefully, and in the sternest tones, "that against the advice of Dr. Horace Frobisher, his superior, he did secretly and stubbornly go ahead with this experiment anyway, without taking the slightest thought as to whether someone might by chance come to that isolated spot, unknown to him, as you boys did. Is this not true, Mistar Brumblydge?"

Prewytt stared back at Towyn.

"This is *not* true, Mr. Towyn Niog. I went out every day to be certain no one was anywhere near, and not an hour before the boys arrived I went out to have a look around. The fact remains that I thought I was alone, and I carried out the experiment in that belief."

But all the bushy eyebrows of the members of the League flattened down once again into straight, severe lines and once again — *scritch, scritch scritch* went their pens, harshly, on the pages in front of them. Then Tyco Bass rose.

"Mr. Prewytt Brumblydge," he said, "all that you have stated, as well as the exhibits we have gathered, will be taken into consideration by the members of the Mycetian League, who will act as the jury. You may expect the results of that consideration to reach you at midnight tonight. The court is now adjourned."

"Miss Brumblydge," said Annabelle Topman,

leaning over to lay her hand on Aunt Matilda's arm while everyone else was getting up and shoving back chairs, "we are the Topmans with whom your nephew has been staying during his illness. We would be so pleased if you would come home and have lunch with us and dinner, too, if you have no other plans."

At this, Aunt Matilda turned in surprise and looked at all the Topmans and Chuck and Cap'n Tom. Then a smile lit her face.

"Prewytt told me all about you in his letter," she said. "And thank you, Mrs. Topman, it would be a great comfort to come with you. I'll have to confess I need some comfort — that scamp — that rascal — *why* wouldn't he listen to me all those years ago when I begged him to put the bones back!"

As for Ta, he conferred with Mr. Bass and the members of the League for a few moments, gave them a sheet of paper, then left and rejoined Mrs. Topman, Dr. Shellworthy, the boys and Cap'n Tom. But he did not say a word about that sheet of paper, nor about what he thought of the trial or of Prewytt's chances.

Through Time and Space

So THEY all went back to the Topmans, except Dr. Shellworthy who had a one o'clock class at the college.

As guests at dinner that night there were of course Ta and Aunt Matilda and Prewytt (who refused to be in the least downcast and seemed, on the whole, well-pleased with how everything had gone), Cap'n Tom and Chuck and, at the last moment, Tyco himself. And he had his gardening coat on as usual instead of that awful, formal jacket he had worn at the trial.

"But, Mr. Bass," exclaimed David, when Tyco appeared suddenly at the front door (having thought himself over from SAGA Hall, but not *right* into the living room for fear of frightening Aunt Matilda who he was quite sure would be there), "Mr. Bass, don't you still have to be considering and weighing and coming to a judgment about Mr. Brumblydge with the rest of the League?"

"Ah, but you see, David," said Tyco, with his arm across David's shoulders as they walked together along the hall toward the living room, "I made up my mind about Prewytt almost at once. And when my good friend, Ta, suggested to us on that sheet of paper what action the court might take in case we found Prewytt guilty in any serious degree, I had no need to consider the matter further. I told the League my thoughts on the subject late this afternoon and then came here at once, leaving them to make up their own minds. They will be influenced by me, of course, but they must talk the matter over from every possible point of view. The League is *very* fair."

Cries of greeting filled the living room, and you would never have imagined that, only a few hours before, Tyco Bass had been the judge sitting in judgment upon Prewytt. How Tyco and Ta and Prewytt talked, for Tyco said he hadn't much time — only until the next morning. Of course Dr. Topman and David and Chuck and Cap'n Tom got some words in edgewise whenever they could, and meanwhile Aunt Matilda insisted on helping Mrs. Topman in the kitchen.

After dinner it was plain that Aunt Matilda was not going to be able to stay awake until midnight to hear the League's judgment on Prewytt. Dr. Topman built up a fine, roaring blaze in the fireplace, and Aunt Matilda, cozy and warm and well-fed, nodded and nodded and finally admitted she would have to be taken to a hotel. But the Topmans said nonsense, that some sort of arrangement could be made right there. And of course Prewytt said he would move out of the guest room and go over to 5 Thallo Street with Tyco. So into the guest room she went, after making them all promise that they would awaken her the minute the verdict arrived.

Well, the moment Aunt Matilda was safely in bed with the light turned out and the windows up, David and Chuck crept by and heard purrings (Aunt Matilda, by her own word, *never* snored). Immediately, they returned to the circle around the fire, consumed with impatience.

"*Now*," said Chuck with relish, "at last we can *really* talk. Mr. Bass, David and I have a story to tell you, and there are some things about it that the Great Ta and Dave and I just don't understand, but we're pretty sure you'll have the answers."

So then the boys told Tyco the whole adventure of their landing in the Lost City of Basidium and of their journey through its ruins, of the miraculous carved paintings and of finding the Mushroom Stones.

"Those people of the Lost City *must* have had

telescopes, Mr. Bass," said Chuck. "But even if they *had* had telescopes, how could they have known about the rings of Saturn when our astronomers only recently found out what they're really made up of? And how could they have known about the expanding universe?"

Now David went and got the Mushroom Stones from his room and the other things he and Chuck had brought back with them.

"Mr. Bass," he said, laying them all in Tyco's lap, "how is it possible that in one little tiny country on earth, the Mycetians have carved the same kind of stones with the same signs on them that a race of Basidiumites thousands and thousands of miles away in space were using?"

Tyco was silent for a moment or two and everybody leaned forward a little, watching his face and waiting in extreme suspense for him to speak.

"I know the answers to all your questions, David and Chuck," he said finally, "and yet I almost hesitate to tell you because it is a story so full of wonder that you may find it hard to believe. I, myself, only learned it during my last stay in M 81 from my brother, who is now living there too, when we were speaking of our family's past.

"You must know, first of all, that I, like Prewytt and like Aunt Matilda, am one of the very Old Ones

216

among Mycetians. But if it startles you to learn that Prewytt was a young man in 1832 when he had that photograph taken with old Morgan Caerwen, then it will no doubt startle you still more to know that I am older than Prewytt by many, many years."

"You *are?*" gasped David.

"But just exactly *how* old, Mr. Bass?" questioned Chuck faintly.

Mr. Bass smiled, and an expression wise and merry and youthful and ancient all at the same time flitted across his small face, and the shadow of it remained in his eyes.

"Let it be sufficient for me to tell you, Chuck and David, that I knew well that famous astronomer, Galileo Galilei."

"*Galileo!*" whispered David.

Dr. Topman stared at Mr. Bass as if he expected him to crumble to dust before his very eyes, and Mrs. Topman went quite pale and put her hand up to her head as if she couldn't possibly have heard correctly.

"But surely," she murmured, "Galileo was born some time in the 1500's."

"That is so," returned Tyco matter-of-factly. "But what I really wanted to tell you is this. A very few Mycetians, some of the Bass family among them, have been given two gifts: one of them the gift of

217

long life, and the other — at the very end of their earthly existence — the gift of being able to think themselves from one place to another, as I am able to do. And when my brother and I were speaking

of this very unusual mode of travel, which does away even with space ships, the story of the Lost City of Basidium and its long-dead inhabitants came out.

"They were a people who, a thousand years ago, knew the exact structure of the solar system at a time when astronomers on this planet still believed that everything revolved around the earth. They knew that the planets are almost round and they understood their movements and the movements of their satellites. They knew that we exist in a great revolving plate of stars, that our sun is near the edge of the plate, and that this plate is only one of millions upon millions of plates, whirlpools and globular masses of suns which we now call galaxies. And they knew that all of these masses or galaxies are rushing away from one another at the rate of millions of miles an hour.

"But it was not because they had invented mighty telescopes and peered into them and figured this all out. You see, they hadn't invented telescopes at all. They had been told of these things by a visitor who had come among them. And this visitor was my grandfather, who also had the gift of traveling by thought from place to place.

"In the beginning," said Tyco, his elbows on the arms of his chair and his long-fingered hands folded together, "the people of the Lost City would not

219

believe my grandfather. They thought he was telling them wonders that he had made up out of his head. But then he taught them how to make a telescope, and when they saw the earth, and how the moon and Basidium revolved around it, and realized that the earth revolves around the sun — why then they believed him, and they thought he was a god. They built a Temple of the Heavens in his honor with those paintings you saw showing all that he had told them about. And they devoted themselves to the study of the heavens, going on and on with the deepest delight in this new adventure he had opened out to them. That temple, David and Chuck, must be the ruin you have described to us."

"But, Mr. Bass, if your grandfather was the visitor who told them all these things," said David, "how, way back a thousand years ago, could *he* have known?"

"Why, because he himself had seen the revolving planets and the moving galaxies, David, just as I have done. He had traveled among them with the swiftness of thought, as I have done.

"As for the Mushroom Stones, the Mycetians of Wales have been carving them for centuries, far back into the past. And when my grandfather told the people of the Lost City about them, they were delighted with the idea — a Mushroom Stone for

220

each family! And so they made their own, and carved on them the designs my grandfather showed them, but also developed others. And of course every family chose its own kind of mushroom. So that is why you found a chest full of these stones. And so it is that still, after all this time, these very same signs and symbols, taken in the first place from Wales to Basidium in my grandfather's mind, are still carved upon the necklaces and possessions of the royal family of Ta."

"Your necklace, Great Ta!" exclaimed David. "That's it! I *knew* — I *knew* —" Ages ago, it seemed to him now, Mr. Bass had first shown him and Chuck and Dr. Shellworthy his own Mushroom Stone. It had been then that David was struck with the question, "Where have I seen those little designs before?" And it had been on the necklace that Ta had given them, that reposed at this very moment in the safe up in Mr. Bass's observatory at 5 Thallo Street.

"It is all so nearly unbelievable," murmured Mrs. Topman, "so *nearly* unbelievable — yet not quite, because it is you who are telling us, Mr. Bass."

"After looking through Tyco's telescope," said Prewytt in a voice that seemed to come from far, far away, "and actually beholding M 81 as *well* as the very solar system in that galaxy where he now lives, I can believe almost anything."

221

At this, Ta gave the strangest little laugh.

"Well, then, Prewytt," he said, getting up all at once and walking back and forth, his hands playing with the jewels of his necklace and his long robes rustling, "if my suggestion to Tyco and the members of the League about your verdict works out as I hope it does, I am glad that you are a sturdy believer. For now you must believe in something else — something that you will be able to accomplish no matter how impossible it seems. However," and here Ta paused in front of Prewytt and gazed upon that little man most thoughtfully, "the League may forgive you entirely. It may let you go scot-free, and then my suggestion will be wasted."

"Your suggestion!" repeated Prewytt, and his face took on a look of mingled suspense, curiosity, and uncertainty. But of course, David thought, being Prewytt Brumblydge's face, curiosity was the most plainly seen.

"Tyco," and Prewytt turned to Mr. Bass, "take pity on me. You know what the suggestion was. Can't you tell me?"

But Tyco did not have to tell him — that is, not ahead of time, for just then there came a knock at the door, in fact three of them: *knock, knock, knock!*

The Judgment

THE sound of those knocks gave everyone the most peculiar feeling up and down his spine, especially as, at the very same moment, the clock on the mantel began chiming midnight. For some reason, not a soul moved until the last of the twelve chimes had struck and died softly away into silence.

Then Tyco went to the door, a few muffled words were heard, and he returned with an envelope and a box, which later proved to contain the Mycetian bones.

"Ah!" said Prewytt. "Now we have it!"

But no one else said anything. The fire flickered on the hearth, making a small sound like a flag flapping in the wind. And in Tyco's hands the fateful envelope crackled and ripped as he tore it open and the sheet of paper inside whispered as he unfolded it. Then he read out the following words:

"If it pleases Ta the King — Ta the Great One — and His Honor Tyco Bass, who presided at the trial of Prewytt M. Brumblydge, held on this day at the Hall of the Society of Anthropologists, Geologists and Archaeologists in Pacific Grove, California, what follows is the judgment on Prewytt Brumblydge handed down by the Members of the Mycetian League after hearing and considering the evidence submitted by the aforesaid Prewytt Brumblydge in answer to the accusations made against him by the League:

"In view of the fact that he deliberately and with full knowledge of what he should have done in the matter, did show a human being the way to the secret burying ground of the Mycetians; did, with this human being, dig up and remove from their appointed resting place three bones; and did persist in keeping in his own possession these bones until such time when he buried them in a foreign place, and

"In view of the fact that he has stubbornly, against the most ancient Mycetian law, refused utterly to return these bones to their appointed resting place, and

"In view of the fact that he deliberately and with full knowledge of the disaster that might have followed had any stranger come into the vicinity of his experiment, did persist in working with an invention of his which he calls a Brumblitron,

"We, the undersigned members of the Mycetian League, do ordain and declare that, under the direction of Tyco Bass, Prewytt M. Brumblydge shall enter the Hole in Space and shall journey through it into the negative universe and shall remain there until he has learned all that it is possible for him to learn with a view to completing his own Brumblydge Theory of the Universe.

Signed, TOWYN NIOG, etc. etc. etc."

David was speechless with horror.

"*The Hole in Space,*" whispered Prewytt.

"*The negative universe* —" burst from Cap'n Tom.

"Enter it *alone?*" cried Mrs. Topman.

Finally Chuck said, when he could get his breath: "Mr. Brumblydge, you don't look a bit scared. Aren't you? We knew a man once, a fellow who used to work up at San Julian — maybe he still does — who went into the Hole in Space by mistake, and he said afterwards he thought he would die. He couldn't have learned anything."

Prewytt, with shining eyes, turned to Ta.

"You remembered what I said to you, didn't you, Your Majesty, in that first conversation of ours?"

"Yes, Prewytt," Ta replied, looking enormously pleased with the way things had turned out, "I did. You expressed the most daring and courageous desire I have ever heard: to travel into the Back of the Beyond, as you call it; and I was determined at some time or another to tell Tyco of your desire, and see what he could do."

"Thank you, Tyco." Prewytt took that slender

225

hand in both of his own short, strong ones. "This will be difficult, but no punishment. It will be a privilege greater than anything I had expected. And don't you worry about me, David and Chuck. Remember that I am not that other fellow — that young, half-baked whippersnapper who works up at San Julian — I am Prewytt Brumblydge. And I shall not leave the Back of the Beyond until I have found the answers to all those questions I have been asking myself in vain since the Brumblydge Theory first began to unfold itself in my head."

There was a small silence, and then Mrs. Topman, looking dazed, got up and went toward the door as if she were going to awaken Aunt Matilda. But Ta held up his hand.

"Wait a moment now," he said. "Prewytt, there is something that must be settled. You know, I appreciate your feelings as a scientist about refusing to take the bones back to the Mycetian burying ground in Wales. But as an inhabitant of a planet where unseen and mysterious forces are deeply respected, I am forced to ask you a question. Prewytt, would you give me the bones in return for whatever Brumblium you receive from me and my people?"

"You actually *want* the plaguy things?" exclaimed Prewytt in astonishment. Ta nodded, and something in his face made Prewytt's eyes twinkle. "No bones, no Brumblium, is that it, Your Majesty?"

Again Ta nodded, and this time a chuckle escaped him. "You see, Prewytt, I intend to return them to the top of the steps near Llanbedr and to bury them there — but, no — come to think of it, I shall have to ask *you* to bury them for me in the precise spot from which you took them. I do hope you can remember where it was, and that you will do me this favor. Surely you will do it — not for yourself, but for me?"

Prewytt burst out laughing and David could have wagered his month's allowance that he saw a flash of relief in the little man's eyes.

"I shall be willing to do more than that, Your Majesty, in return for all the Brumblium I'll be asking of you."

Now they awakened Aunt Matilda, as they had promised to do, and told her the verdict was that Prewytt had to go on a long journey in order to learn more about his Theory of the Universe. And when she asked if it were a difficult and dangerous journey, they had to say yes, it was. But they were certain, they added, that as Tyco was planning it and was even going part way, Prewytt would return from it safely. So she sighed and went back to sleep because she was used to Prewytt's gallivanting, and

227

there was nothing she could do about it one way or the other.

Very early the next morning, long before Aunt Matilda was up, all of them — the Topmans and Cap'n Tom and Chuck and Mr. Bass and Ta and Prewytt Brumblydge — went down to the space ship on Cap'n Tom's beach. And the plan of travel was this:

Ta and Prewytt and Tyco would take the space ship to Wales, bury the bones, and then go on to Basidium. There Tyco and Prewytt would have a good, long visit with Mr. Theo, and pick up more Brumblium. Then Tyco would take off with Prewytt for the Hole in Space, see him safely into it, and then think himself to his home in M 81. First, however, he would set the controls of the space ship so that Prewytt could direct it back to Earth the moment he was ready to come.

David and Chuck kept shouting and waving happily as the silver ship took off into the gray-blue dawn sky. But though Annabelle Topman waved, she could not seem to get out a sound. And David had a feeling that perhaps his mother had just been through too much lately for one who had never, before their meeting with Tyco Bass, had anything to weigh on her mind but Cub Scouts and her family and the Garden Club and the World Affairs Council.

Months later, after Prewytt had returned from the Hole in Space and had successfully set up his Brumblitrons on a large scale near the sea, where they turned thousands of gallons of sea water into fresh, he went into hibernation at 5 Thallo Street. Here he started to write out the whole of his Brumblydge Theory of the Universe. And he told David and Chuck that his only regret was that he could not, for years to come, publish the true story of how he had at last found the answers to all his questions.